Bonefish Blues

Will Service Adventures

Steven Becker

* * *

Join my mailing list

and get a free copy of Wood's Ledge

http://mactravisbooks.com

Chapter 1

Joey Pagliano opened the trunk and pulled the body onto the gravel driveway.

"That's the third one this month," Eli Braken said as he puffed furiously on his cigar to cover the smell of the bloated body. "We can't keep dumping your trash out there."

Pagliano ignored him and went to the storage room. "Did you get the ice like I asked or are you just going to stand there and preach?" He emerged with a large canvas bag used to preserve tournament fish.

Braken opened the trunk of the Cadillac and removed two bags of ice and set them next to the body. "Just saying. We have plans for that island. You keep bringing bodies down here and someone finds out, it could blow the whole deal."

Pagliano tried to control his temper. Dumping bodies in Miami had gotten tricky. In the past he had taken his victims out to the Everglades, but the once deserted swamp had turned into an eco-tourist park in the last few years. Cement shoes had gone out of vogue as well with South Beach's resurgence. You couldn't get out of one of the cuts leading to the Atlantic without a tourist training their binoculars on you. Even the backwaters of Homestead were constantly patrolled by Fish and Game officers.

The Gulf side of the Keys was too vast to patrol and tourists rarely ventured onto the unmarked shoal ridden shallows. Flamingo Key was the best option whether Braken liked it or not. The deserted island with its abandoned septic tanks was the perfect dumping spot.

"Cody's out on a charter. We won't be able to dump it until tomorrow."

"Just shut up and help me," Pagliano said as he dragged the body toward the bag. Braken reluctantly came over to help stuff the body in. They added ice and lifted it into the trunk. "Not like he's not dead already."

* * *

The fin sliced through the water as the fish cruised the flat. Will saw it before the man did, his view from the poling platform of the flats boat giving him an advantage. "There," he whispered, as if the fish could hear him from fifty feet. "Lead him with the fly."

The fly line was pooled on the deck around the man's feet. Will grimaced, already knowing the outcome but unable to correct him, as the man lifted line off the water and swung the rod back over his head for the back cast. The line whipped too far back and snagged in the mangroves lining the shore of the small island known as Flamingo Key. Frustrated, he looked at Will, "I can't get this right."

Will poled the boat toward the bank to retrieve the fly, shaking his head; the fish was gone. "It's hard. But when you hook that first fish, it'll all be worth it." The boat edged toward the bush where the fly was snagged and he gently reached over, pulling the offending branch toward him and removing the hook. Pole in hand, he moved the boat toward the feeding fish. "Let's do a couple more practice casts off to the side. Get your rhythm back."

He moved the boat farther away from the mangroves and nosed it into the current. Another boat, all too familiar to him, was fishing a quarter mile off the point. It had the familiar outline of a cuddy cabin; probably Cody Braken's Grady-White. Will wondered why Cody fished that spot so often. He had checked it out; the bottom was sandy there, barren of the rocks or coral that attracted fish. He knew Cody was lazy, but there was no way someone with his experience as a charter captain would fish there. He squinted into the sun and watched them; rods bent over, rejoicing as the fish came over the side of the boat. He shrugged his shoulders and wondered again what made that spot so special.

The line snapped back and forth as the man practiced, bringing him back to the present. Will watched with feigned interest. He'd been here and done that with rookie anglers for years. Fly fishing was not rocket science, but it took practice. A thousand good casts and you had a chance at being somewhat competent. It was playing the law of averages. He knew the man would eventually get a good cast to the right spot, and — fish gods willing — hook the fish. He looked up at the cloudless sky, the color a pale blue, perfectly accenting the water, and hoped the gods had heard his plea. As if on cue, the man pulled back on the rod, lucky not to pull the hook from the fish.

"Got one!" he said.

Will's eyes followed the fluorescent green fly line to where it disappeared in the water. He watched several feet of line peel off the rod as the fish ran. The dorsal fin rose as it dove attempting to shake the hook. Satisfied it was hooked well, he moved his gaze toward the rod. The nine-weight rod was bent double but was suitable for the task.

"Easy, don't yank on it. That's a nice fish, and you're going to have to fight it on the reel." The man looked at him, confused, line pooled at his feet. "Loosen up your right hand and let him take some line if he wants, while you reel the extra line on with your left hand." Often smaller fish could be brought in by hand-lining the loose line. In this case, Will knew the angler would need the assistance of the drag the reel provided to tire the fish enough to land it.

The man returned his gaze to the reel. His right hand, holding the line pinched against the rod, eased slightly, allowing the fish to take some line and run instead of meeting resistance and either breaking off or shaking the hook.

Will noticed the fish start to sense the lack of pressure. "A little harder, and bring the rod to the side a little, not overhead." He watched as the man followed his directions. It would be a constant adjustment of give and take until the man had the line on the reel and the mechanical drag could take over. Until then, the inexperienced angler would have to sense when to loosen and tighten the line against the rod as the fish moved. Either too loose or too tight, and the fish would be gone. Slowly, the man got comfortable with his right hand and started winding the line on the deck onto the reel with his left. Will breathed a sigh of relief once all the line was on the reel and the angler was able to fight the fish with the assistance of the reel's drag.

"Got him now," the man exclaimed, relief evident in his voice.

He adjusted the drag and started to bring the fish toward the boat. Now, when it wanted to run, the drag set on the reel handled it evenly. It took several long minutes before they could see a flash of silver come parallel with the boat, and when it did, Will kneeled on the deck and reached both hands in the water.

"Okay, step back with the rod and bring him to me."

The man took two steps backward as the fish slid over Will's waiting hands. Once it was above both open palms, he raised them and plucked the fish from the water, then grabbed the mouth of the twenty-four-inch fish and held it for the man to see. The crimson scales glittered in the sun, the dark spot above the tail easily identifying it as a redfish.

"Wow. Nice fish, and damned more fun than catching it on a spinning reel with a dead bait on the end of the line."

Those were the words Will longed to hear. They made his career as a charter captain worthwhile — justification for everything he did bringing novice fly fishermen out, tying their flies on the line, managing tangles and removing wayward hooks. He held the mouth pinched between two fingers and went to his belt for his pliers. The fly pulled easily from the fish's mouth, and he handed it back to the happy angler.

"Lefty's Deceiver. Works every time." With that, the fish went into the box. Flats fishing in the Florida Keys brought in both edible and sport fish, the redfish a very desirable catch. A quick look to the west showed the sun about a hand and a half above the horizon; roughly an hour and a half until it set.

The man followed his gaze, grinning. "That made my day. We can head in anytime."

Will knew better than to push too far. Pulling the plug and heading in after a catch was the best way to end a charter. If they continued, the man would quickly forget the thrill of the catch after another inevitable mess of tangled line ensued; and that would certainly ruin the day.

He breathed out, knowing they'd been fortunate to hook up this close to slack tide. Pulling the twenty-foot push pole used to move the boat through the shallow water from its deck fitting, where it had been anchoring the boat against the gentle current, he secured the pole in it's holder, went to the console and started the engine. One hand pushed the throttle forward as the other turned the wheel toward the west. Seconds later, the wind blew through his hair as the boat went up onto plane, skimming over the small waves. The flats of Flamingo Key receded behind them.

Russell Key was the first landmark, with Stirrup Key jutting out in the distance. Will held the course straight from the shallow flat off Bamboo Key to Stirrup Key. There he turned the wheel to the left and ran parallel with the mainland. Once past the airport, he slowed the boat and turned toward a small canal. The man-made canals, blasted in the 1960s and 70s, provided access to many of the areas that had been previously landlocked by shallow water.

"Got a couple of beers in the cooler," he shouted to his client.

"Sure, sounds good," the man said, gratefully reaching down and grabbing a dripping can of Yuengling. "Took me a while to get the hang of it, but that was everything I expected and more. What a rush."

Will let the man revel in his victory as he navigated the canal. The boat idled to the dock where he skillfully cut the engine, reached over for the line sitting on the dock and tied the boat off. He heard the sound of another boat approaching, too fast as usual, and knew Cody was back.

Chapter 2

The Grady-White pulled in too fast, the wake from the twenty-two-foot hull rocking the other boats in the marina. Will was thrown off balance and his customer off his feet, almost over the transom. *The Kraken* in bold letters written on the stern of the offending boat stared him in the face.

"What's with the jerk?" the angler asked.

"Never mind him. Let's go on up to the shade and settle up," Will replied.

"Y'all catch anything?" Cody yelled as he swung his boat toward the dock. "Yo, Matt, grab the line dude." He tossed the blood-stained line toward a boy on the deck. "Tie her up. I'll toss up the fish."

Matt tied the line to the forward cleat and waited for Cody to toss the stern line. Instead, Cody reached into the cooler. "To the victors go the spoils." He recited the standard line as he handed beers around.

The tide pulled on the boat, moving the back end away from the dock, but Cody was passing out beers - not aware of the movement. The boat was almost perpendicular when he realized what was happening and tossed the other line out. It flattened on the water, falling two feet short of the dock. Matt got on his belly, reached out for the line, and pulled the boat in.

"Hurry up. Got a cooler full of fish for you to clean." Cody reached into the fish box and started tossing carcasses onto the dock. Matt lined up the assortment of grouper and snapper in size order setting up for the requisite picture. He picked the two largest for the men to hold.

9

The men helped each other onto the dock, each swaying slightly. Another epic day on Cody's boat to tell their friends about. They grinned and bumped fists as the boy laid out the catch.

"What the hell, boy?" one asked as Matt started throwing fish into the water.

"They're short. Snappers've got to be twelve inches, groupers twenty." Three more fish followed.

"You could hurry your ass up and just clean them. Toss the carcasses, nobody'll be the wiser," Cody said as he hopped to the dock, catching himself on a piling to break his fall.

Matt ignored him and handed each angler one of the larger fish. "Be happy to take a picture for you. Won't take long to clean them after that."

Bellies poked out of shirts and well-chewed cigar stubs hung from their mouths as the men pushed their hats back, took off their sunglasses, and smiled.

"What's that all about?" the man with Will asked as he handed him two hundred dollar bills.

Will peeled the perfect fillet off the back side of the redfish and tossed the translucent spine to a waiting pelican. "Here you go." He handed the bagged fillets to the man. "Good fishing with you."

The man looked down at his catch, then glanced toward the scene on the dock. Will followed his look knowing he had some buyer's remorse. "There's no skill in that. Anyone can go out, drink some beers, soak some bait, and bring back fish. Catching them on a fly, just taking what you need for dinner ... I'd say that's a whole lot more honorable. Those guys don't respect what we've got here. Without sportsmen like you, this place'll be wiped out in a few years. Damned shame."

The man shook his head and walked toward the dock, passing Matt as he navigated the narrow gangplank separating the seawall from the floating dock. Will watched as he walked up to the group, accepted a beer, and listened intently to their tale. He hung around for a while, finally taking a business card from Cody.

"Never mind that. You're doing it the right way." Ned put a cold soda on the cleaning table and watched Will as he finished hosing off the table's surface and dock below. The old man had been around the Keys for years. A former college professor turned marina owner, he was the go-to guy for any local knowledge. He'd been there, done that and now held court at his dockside, liberally spreading his advice to anyone who would listen. "Takes a while to build a reputation here. I've been watching them come and go for thirty years." He pointed to the dock. "That boy—" He tilted his head toward Cody. "Without his daddy, he'd be cleaning your fish. The old man puts the customers in his boat."

"Sometimes it looks like I have to do everything the hard way," Will said.

"There's only two ways, and the hard way is usually the right way. Besides, I don't see you drinking beers and talking trash like that six days a week. That's no way to live."

Will wondered if Ned knew how lonely his nights were.

Matt walked up holding a basket full of fish in his hands, "Can I take that table?"

"Sure. I'm finished." Will stepped to the side.

Matt set the laundry basket of fish on the deck, grabbed an empty bucket, and set the hose in it. While it was filling he took the sharpening steel to the worn fillet knife. One at a time he skillfully cleaned the fish, placing the fillets in the bucket of water, popping the eyes out of the carcass and tossing them to the waiting birds.

"Take the soda." Will pushed the unopened can toward him.

Matt wiped the sweat from his brow and cracked the tab. "Thanks, Will. My dad only has beer on the boat."

Will and Ned watched the boy finish cleaning the fish. He

hosed the table off, wiping the remnants through the drain hole, and carefully took the fillets out of the bucket. Separated by species, he started to bag them, sucking the air from each bag before sealing it.

"What are you being so careful for?" Ned asked. "Not like those guys'll appreciate the effort you're taking."

"Just hoping for a big tip. Saving up for a car."

* * *

Will stood by watching, as Cody and the two men approached. Matt handed them the bucket, baggies neatly stacked on the bottom, a scoop of ice on top to keep them cold. "Here you go, sir."

He waited, looking up at them expectantly.

"Go on down and clean the boat now," Cody told him.

The men ignored Matt's glance as he headed down toward the dock, and Cody turned back to Will.

"Yo, Will. Didn't do so hot today. Just a red?"

"Released a couple of nice bones and a small tarpon."

"Don't have much interest in that whole release thing." Cody elbowed one of the men in the side. "Know what I mean, boys? That there's a good day's fishing." He looked at the bucket. "Maybe ought to tip the boy something for cleaning them for you." He accepted a twenty, and exchanged handshakes and fist bumps with his two clients. "See ya'll at the bar."

Then he turned back to Will and Ned. "Another banner day, boys," he said. He winked, pocketed the bill, and headed towards the boat.

"You going to pass that on?" Will called, referring to the bill in Cody's pocket.

"Don't think that's any of your business. It's my boy. You looking to clean my fish? Maybe pick up a few extra bucks? Charters ain't exactly lining up for you." Cody glanced toward the dock, scowling. "Tell the boy I'm not waiting for him. I'm heading for the bar. He can walk over when he's done. Tell him I'll let him practice his driving on the way home."

Will shook his head. "Yeah, I'll tell him." He watched Cody with disdain as he walked toward the dock. Matt had his shirt off, sweat mixing with soap as he scrubbed the boat. "Hey, take a break and let it soak." He looked over the bloodstained deck and frowned. "Raw water sprayer not working? Wouldn't be half as bad if he sprayed it down a few times when they're out there."

Matt put down the brush and picked up the soda. He took a long sip. "You know the old man. Says it's all part of the effect." He put down the drink, picked up the brush, and started scrubbing again.

Will checked his dock lines. His twenty-one-foot Action Craft flats boat sat still in the water, the tide slack. He hopped onto the deck and started stowing gear. A quick freshwater spray, and the boat was clean. He was religious about spraying after each fish, although that wasn't as often as some of his charters would like. It burned him that the man from today had taken a card from Cody. He'd read the guy wrong. Maybe should have chummed up some snappers and let him take a limit. You could still catch them on the fly. Maybe his business would be better if he let the anglers catch their limit, but conservation was wired into him, his reputation built on catch and release and he often wrongly assumed his charters knew that before they went out.

The two months of tarpon season were different. He was the man then; tarpon was a release only fishery. Even Cody wouldn't take tarpon — wouldn't even fish for them. Will was booked solid during the season, but slower the rest of the year. But it seemed that since the economy had died, folks had lost interest in catch and release. They were all about filling their freezers. Bonefish and permit, the other catch and release fish, were sought by a more exclusive, though dwindling group. He thought about his bank account, currently as low as a spring tide.

Matt was coiling the hose on the dock when Will passed by. He paused and looked at the boy. He reached into his pocket and took out a twenty. It wasn't right how Cody treated him, "Here. That's from those guys your dad took out today. Said to meet him at the bar when you're done."

"Thanks, Will. I don't get too many tips." He pocketed the money, put his shirt on, and headed toward the building.

"Saw you give the boy some cash," Ned said, approaching.

"You know Cody is drinking on that tip money right now. He's a good kid. Doesn't deserve to be treated like that."

"Yeah, he is. But he's not your responsibility. You can't save everything. When was the last time you went out and had a good time?"

Will just looked at him, saying nothing in acknowledgment. Ned took the cue and went back to the office.

Chapter 3

"Give me seven points and I'll take Vanderbilt," Cody said, taking a long draw off his beer. He looked up at the flat screen behind the bar; the talking heads on the screen had all picked Georgia. Cody knew he was going out on a limb, but the only way to dig himself out of the hole he was in was with a big shovel and the odds on Vanderbilt winning would buy him a backhoe. A win here would settle all his debts — he ignored the consequences of what a loss would do.

The local bookie sat next to him, sipping a soda, "Number one, you got no credit. Number two, are you out of your mind?" Cody followed the man's gaze to the screen.

He reached into his pocket and pulled out the twenty. "Here, let's call this a down payment. Make the bet a hundred," he said trying to keep the look of desperation off his face.

The man grabbed the twenty. "You ain't got that kind of credit. But, I'll take your twenty."

Cody guzzled the rest of his beer and slammed the mug down on the bar. "Just you wait. I'll find another bookie and you'll be missin' my business." He turned and looked around the bar for someone else he could bet with.

The man saw what he was up to. "Good luck there. In this pisshole of a town, I'm the only game. I'll take your action. Just make sure your old man backs you up."

Cody stared at the screen, the kickoff seconds away. *What the hell,* he thought. His old man would bail him out. Not that he'd need it, he reassured himself. He ordered another beer and watched the game unfold. He got up at halftime, needing a bathroom break after half a dozen beers. His hopes were in the gutter; Vanderbilt was down by fourteen. Back at the bar, and ready for the third quarter, he switched to bourbon. The chasm deepened to twenty points early in the fourth quarter. Defeated, he finally left the bar.

* * *

Matt was texting, his head down, when Cody approached the car. His math book was in his lap, a notepad open on the seat next to him. He jumped when Cody opened the door and got in. "Hey, Dad."

"Hey, yourself. What are you doing on that stupid phone?" He grabbed it and slammed it on the dashboard. "You need to be working those books," he slurred.

Matt looked him over, knowing he was drunk and had probably lost money by his temper. "Why don't you let me drive?"

"I got this," Cody mumbled as he turned the key. The engine turned over, and Matt reached for the keys.

"Dad, I've got my permit, and you've been drinking. I'll drive. One more DUI and you have to do jail time," Matt made a move for the door but was too late.

Cody ignored him and pulled the lever down. He was sloppy drunk, and jerked too hard moving the shifter past reverse and into drive.

"Dad, stop!"

But it was too late; the truck jerked forward, slamming into the parking bumper. Matt grabbed his books and phone and reached for the door handle. "You can't drive like this. I'll walk." He got out and slammed the door, leaping out of the way as Cody found reverse and pulled out of the lot, tires shooting crushed coral at him.

Head down he walked to the curb. Books at his feet, he sat on the vacant parking bumper and stared at his phone. It was five miles to his mom's house. He was supposed to be staying with his dad this week, but he had no wish to be around the old man any more than necessary, especially when he was like this. She would always let him stay there. Just as he started to dial her number, he saw Will pull into the lot and he set down the phone. The old pickup stopped next to him.

"Hey, you okay?" Will asked.

"Yeah, sure. Just need a ride. I was just going to call my mom."

"No problem. I'll take you over there. You eat anything yet? I was just about to get something." He figured Matt had been here the whole time waiting for Cody, "Want to go?"

Matt's stomach had been grumbling for hours, but his dad had never asked whether he was hungry. The fact that Will did brought up a lump in his throat, and he quickly swallowed it down. "Yeah, that'd be great." He went toward the rusted door and got in.

Will pulled out onto US1 and headed north. "Where's your dad?"

"Think he had too much to drink again. Took off." Matt put his head down and stared at the seat. They drove in silence. It was strange how Will was always nicer to him than his own dad. Will was someone who he could count on, although he'd never really tested the trust. It was just nice to have someone that did stuff for you; knew when you needed help and when you needed to be left alone. He'd never seen Will drunk or abusive either.

"Barbeque okay?" Will broke the silence as he pulled into the parking lot.

"Oh, sure."

The place was quiet. Thursday nights in November were slow. The summer crowds had left and the snow birds would not start arriving until after Thanksgiving. They ordered ribs, filled their soda cups, sat down and ate. They didn't talk much as they plowed through the food, watching the end of the game as Georgia rolled Vanderbilt 42-7. "Do you even drink?" Matt asked, watching Will sip his iced tea.

"Sometimes, but nothing good comes of that. Learned that lesson a long time ago. I'll have a beer once in a while, but--" He stopped.

"Yeah, I know. My dad drinks too much." Matt's eyes teared. He got up, took both trays and dumped them in the trash, turning away so that Will would not see his face.

"Staying with your mom?" Will asked as they pulled back out on the road.

"Supposed to be with my dad this week, but he's drunk and mad. My mom said when he got like that I should stay with her. She's trying to get the custody thing changed, but she says my grandpa has too much clout here."

"No worries. I'll run you over there." Matt watched the road as Will turned off US1 toward the Gulf side. The houses were dark, vegetation taking over many of the yards. Twice he hesitated and had to ask Matt for directions. After several turns they pulled into a small driveway. The house stood on wooden stilts, clapboard siding in need of maintenance, probably built in the 1950s, like many of the houses in this area. A light was on in a back room.

Will paused, then turned to Matt. "Hey, you good? I'll wait till you get in."

Matt opened the door and got out, "Thanks for the ride and dinner," he said as he closed the door and went for the stairs, wishing he could talk to him more about his dad.

"Hey, hang in there," Will called after him.

Matt walked the unlit path to the stairs. A security light came on as he hit the first tread illuminating the steps and front porch. Before he reached the top, the door opened and his mother appeared in a bathrobe. Matt went to her for a long hug.

* * *

Will saw the tears roll down her attractive face, illuminated by the security light, and watched as Matt went in. The woman remained, squinting past the light at him. She put up a hand with a finger extended, asking him to wait, and then went inside, the door closing behind her. Will sat in the truck, wondering what she wanted, not wanting to get involved. Matt talked about her occasionally, but he'd never met her.

Then the door opened and she reappeared. He watched as she walked down the stairs and followed the path of the headlights to the truck. The bathrobe was gone; in its place she wore tight jeans and a white t-shirt. The tears were gone as well, and her auburn hair was brushed.

He rolled down the window as she approached. "Hi, I'm Will."

"I know," she said. "Matt talks about you all the time. Thought it was time I met you." She leaned in toward him with a smile, close enough for him to smell the freshly applied perfume. "I want to thank you for looking after him. His dad's not very responsible."

Will looked at her his silence prompting a response.

"Okay, he's an irresponsible ass. Anyway, my name's Nicole," she smiled again stepping back slightly, turning her hips so he could see her body.

He couldn't help but notice and with his eyes on her breasts he blurted, "I'm Will," realizing he'd already introduced himself he tried to recover, "But, I guess you know that."

"Maybe I'll see you around some time — thanks for looking after him," she said. Before he could say anything else, she leaned into the car and kissed his cheek, turned and walked away.

The sway in her walk kept his attention as she went up the stairs. The door closed and he sat there for a long second before backing out of the driveway. The roads were dark and he missed the turn, his mind preoccupied. Finally back on the main street, he drove toward the glow of lights marking US1. He turned back toward the Gulf side and went half a mile before turning again. Several turns later, he pulled up to a gate with an old building permit box next to it. Getting out, he opened the latch on the rusted farm gate. It swung unevenly as he opened it. He got back in and pulled the truck through leaving the gate open behind him.

He drove past several piles of construction materials before pulling up to the dark house. Built on concrete piers, the cinder block walls were waiting for stucco, but otherwise the house looked finished. Driftwood beams and fascia accented the windows and doors in a style that set the house apart from the other cookie cutter houses. Using the flash on his phone to light the way, he admired his work as he walked upstairs. The unfinished, handmade door opened and he entered the dark house. Still holding the phone for light, he went to a hurricane lamp and lit the wick with the lighter sitting next to it. The light glowed brighter as the wick sucked oil, soon illuminating the room.

The kitchen was off to the left, with hand planed cypress cabinets installed. The counters were still plywood sheets. A small propane refrigerator sat next to a camp stove in the spaces where the permanent appliances would go. The rest of the room was open, with a bare plywood floor. Cypress beams and planks highlighted the ceiling as well as the window and door surrounds. Part carpenter, part fisherman he had done all the woodwork himself. Carpentry was a passion, much like fly fishing, but where he could find work as a fishing guide, he had trouble finding work as a carpenter. His reputation for insisting on doing only custom work and doing it his way turned people away. People always liked what he did, but didn't want to pay the artist price tag. He opened the French doors, which led out to a deck. The Gulf was visible through the hand carved boards in the railing, waves shimmering, lit by the quarter moon. The small Honda generator started with one pull, and several lights flickered and then came on as the generator evened out.

The house was ready for paint, and had been for awhile. It was livable now, with the exception of the power situation. He had water and gas, but he was at odds with the power company, who had turned off his temporary service when his permit had expired last year. They refused to hook up permanent power until he had a final occupancy permit. He was capable of doing the rest of the work, but unlike carpentry he had little interest.

At the table, he waited for his laptop to boot up. The old operating system took time, and he thought about Nicole while he waited. It had been a long time since a woman had shown interest in him. Finally the home screen showed, and he opened his email, hoping a charter had booked for tomorrow, or there was at least an inquiry. There was nothing there, so he closed the cover, turned off the generator, and went to bed.

He lay awake unable to sleep. Though he lived in the capital of mellow, he had a reputation for having less ambition than most. There was real passion buried inside him; carpentry or fly fishing, but neither did a good job of paying the bills, Maybe he should do meat charters, or take a real job, at least put enough money in the bank to finish the house, get a girl, start a family. Finally he drifted off to an unsettled sleep.

Chapter 4

With no charter for the day, and the weather favorable, Will paddled toward Flamingo Key, a small hump in the distance. Sunlight danced on the small ripples of the Gulf, the water not quite flat calm, but dappled with small wind waves. He paddled easily through the early morning slack tide, his paddleboard sliding through the water. Sunrise was his favorite time to be on the water, before the heat and activity of the day set in. He looked behind him every few minutes, checking the fishing line trailing behind the board. Every so often, a flats boat cruised parallel to them. This early, they were usually charters and the captains respected the paddlers, leaving enough distance so that their wakes would not effect them. Later in the day when the tourists came out, it would be a different story.

Next to him in a kayak was Roc Bennet, a contractor friend. Roc tagged along any chance he got, trading advice on fishing for help with Will's house. Both men knew who came out better on the deal. Roc got to fish with a guide once or twice a week, and it had been more than a month since Will had even hinted that he needed help with his house.

He planned the five-mile paddle around the tide. A strong current or wind would make it a harder outing, especially for Will on the stand up board. But that was part of the game. He'd come prepared. His board was outfitted for fishing, utilizing a milk crate bungeed to the front and a cooler behind him. The rod was in a holder screwed to reinforcement in the deck.

They stroked easily, talking quietly as they paddled. Will

wanted to say something about the scene at the dock and meeting Nicole the night before, but thought better of it. Roc was a trusted friend and sounding board, but this felt too much like gossip. He hated the coconut telegraph, as the locals referred to the network prevalent through the Keys. One too many times, he had been on the wrong side of it, usually at Cody's doing.

He had grown up with Cody. Through high school they ran in different circles; never friends, but never enemies either. After graduation, Will had seen and heard of Cody's exploits, but through their twenties and into their thirties they had no contact. Will had been more motivated then, before the setbacks of life slowed him down. Working as a carpenter during the week and a mate for fishing charters had allowed him to save enough to buy his own boat and take a shot a being his own boss. Cody on the other hand had never amounted to much, but didn't seem to suffer for it. Old man Braken had bought him the Grady-White and shuttled clients his way whenever he could to supplement the off the books kind of work he had him do on the side. From the first glimpse of recognition that day on the docks several years ago when Will pulled up in the slightly used Action Craft there had been tension between them. *Maybe the competition,* Will thought. *Or maybe because Matt gravitated towards him rather than his father.*

Instead, he and Roc talked football, fishing, and the inevitable slow economy. Both men had been adversely affected when things went south several years earlier. The building industry was just now getting back on its feet, five years later, but fly fishing was still way down. These days, many fishermen preferred to try and offset the cost of the charter with a freezer full of fish.

Suddenly the reel on his board spun.

"You've got something!" Roc yelled.

Will turned and looked at the rod, which was bent over, line spilling off the spinning reel. He set the paddle on the board

23

between his legs and carefully turned on the thirty-two-inch-wide board until he could sit on the cooler and reach behind him for the rod. Once in hand, he tightened the drag, slowing the line, and held the rod high.

"'Bet it's a 'cuda," he said, as he started to recover line. Although not good table fare, the foot-long barracudas that prowled the flats were fun to catch. It didn't take him long to bring the fish to the boat. Rod held high over his head, he reached for the line and grabbed the leader a foot above the fish, then set the rod back in the holder and reached for the pliers clipped to his belt. The steel jaws clamped down on the hook and he shook the fish off, careful to avoid the teeth, which could take off a finger.

The fish had interrupted their conversation and they paddled the half hour to Flamingo Key in silence, the only sound was their paddles dipping in and out of the water.

"Set up over there," Will called to Roc, pointing to a clump of mangroves a hundred feet off. "Go in close to shore and cast toward the deeper water." He pointed to the darker line of water running parallel to the Key, then waited until Roc was set up, and watched for a few minutes as he started casting, double hauling, letting more line out with each cast.

Satisfied, he paddled toward the point of the Key closest to land. It was a hard channel to fish, but the rewards were great. It wasn't very often a charter client was skilled enough to fish the tricky intersection between the wind, current and tide here. He had better luck with the novices where he had Roc set up, on the leeward side of the Key and out of the wind and current. He reached around for the fly rod and started casting, letting the board drift in the current. He got four casts off with no fish before the current pulled him past the channel. He put down the rod and paddled back up current, patiently starting in the same spot. It took five drifts before he hooked a nice bonefish. Several more followed, all released.

The rod was back in its holder and he was about to check on Roc when he saw the boat barreling directly toward them. He winced when it passed a shallow sandbar; they were either very lucky, or the captain knew that it was only passible at high tide. The boat was close enough now to see the shape of the Grady-White. What was Cody doing running over that bottom? The waters of the Gulf side were riddled with banks and shoals, many unmarked.

Wary of the intruders, he paddled around the Key, just out of sight, and watched from the cover of some mangroves as they approached. The wake reached him just as the boat slowed, and a flock of birds flew screeching from the mangroves as the waves crashed against the shore. The only noise now was the idle of the motor and the waves hitting the sand. Then he heard the voice.

"Look at it? Freakin' paradise. Great flats, not too far out, and the clearing in the center would be perfect for a half dozen houses. You could put a dock over there and power up the whole enchilada with some solar cells and a windmill," boomed the voice.

Will cringed. He knew that voice, audible across the fifty feet of water, and the man it belonged to. Cody's father, Eli Braken, or Judge Braken, as he preferred to be called. The retired judge was now a self-proclaimed real estate mogul. He sat back on the cooler, gripping the paddle blade stuck in the sand as an anchor, listening to him wax on about his vision for Flamingo Key. The splash of a paddle breaking water alerted him to Roc's presence. Not wanting to be seen, he lifted his paddle from the sand, paddled quietly toward the kayak and motioned for Roc to follow around the backside of the island.

"What's up?" Roc asked when they stopped. They had to take a few strokes every so often to counteract the current and remain in place. The water here was too deep to set their paddles as brakes, and the tide tugged them away from land.

Will turned toward his friend. "That was Braken and another dude in that boat over there. He's talking like he wants to sell the island. I don't even think he owns it." He wondered if the island was Braken's to sell or if it was just another scam the old man had cooked up. "Why the heck would you want to build on this pile of sand anyway?"

Roc was about to answer when they heard the roar of the outboard, a thump, and a man yell.

"What the hell was that?" Will yelled, starting to paddle toward the noise. They had to fight the current now, but with urgency in their strokes they traversed the quarter-mile-long Key in a few minutes. The silt trail left by the outboard was visible well before they rounded the point.

"What's that?" Roc asked.

"Bet they grounded. The old man ought to know better than that. Let's see if anyone's hurt." He paddled around the point toward the source of the sediment, where he saw the hull beached on a sandbar a few feet from the Key, its engine still revving, the propeller the source of the silt as it churned up the sand in an attempt to free the boat.

"Hey, shut the engine off. You're just spinning your wheels!" Will yelled as he approached. The men ignored him as he paddled close enough to see that no one was hurt, then turned to go.

"Don't believe in helping out your neighbors?" Braken's voice echoed toward him. He turned back to the man.

"You shouldn't be here. It's way too shallow for the draft on that boat. Where's Cody? He'd know better."

Braken ignored the question, "Was an accident, son. My friend here slipped and hit the throttle." He winked at the driver.

Will looked at Braken as the boat revved again. He was chomping a cigar butt, pushing back and forth on the throttle. He shifted his glance towards Braken, "Tell him to stop and I'll help you out." He regretted it the minute it was out of his mouth, but he couldn't stand to see the damage to the pristine flat continue.

Braken shouted at the driver, who yelled something back that Will couldn't understand over the roar of the engine. He paddled to the boat, kneeled down, and got off the board. A hard shove pinned the board's fin in the sand to anchor it, and he hopped the gunwale, landing easily on the bloodstained deck of the Grady-White.

Braken was leaning against the transom, clearly distancing himself from the driver. Will went to the wheel and tapped the man on the shoulder. He found himself on the deck seconds later after a quick right cross came out of nowhere. No one moved to help him.

The driver turned with a scowl. Will wouldn't soon forget the scar on his brow, pulsing like a vein. "Do not touch me. People who think they can touch me don't do it twice."

Will got up from the deck, rubbing the sore spot on his jaw. As he rose, he noticed a large canvas bag in the cabin — the same kind of bag used to store trophy fish before tournament weigh-ins. This one was large enough for a marlin. Several five-gallon buckets were strapped down beside it. He turned to Braken, shrugged his shoulders, and waited for him to intervene. But the only sound was the revving of the engine.

"Listen. Tide will be cresting in an hour. You only need a couple of inches and she'll float it off," he mumbled and jumped out of the boat. Seconds later he was back on his board paddling away, the sound of the engine breaking the solitude of the flat.

Will couldn't help but think as he paddled. He was curious about Braken's plans to sell the island and the fish bag nagged at him, but he did what he always did and put it out of his mind.

Chapter 5

"What was that guy's problem?" Roc asked.

"Don't know. Pretty scary-looking dude, though," Will said as they paddled toward the boat ramp. "What I want to know is what Braken is up to. I can't seem to get away from him and his son. Don't know which one gets under my skin faster."

They paddled in silence, the wind at their backs, quickly gaining on the 54th Street boat ramp. Will went to his knees just before the nose of the board hit the concrete of the ramp, hopped off, and lifted the board onto the pavement, careful not to ding the delicate fiberglass. Roc followed, less careful with the molded plastic kayak, and went for his truck. They unloaded gear from the boats, placed it in the back of the truck and lashed the kayak and board down to the truck's rack.

Roc reached into a cooler in the backseat and pulled out a couple of beers. "Want one?"

"Yeah, actually maybe more than one," Will said. He usually passed on the after-paddle beer, but the cold bottle felt good against the bruise forming on his chin. He pulled it away from his jaw, twisted off the cap, took a long sip, and placed the bottle back against his face.

Roc watched him closely. "What're you going to do about Braken?"

"I'm going to buy Cody a few beers and see if I can get him talking. I want to see if he knows what the old man is up to. He fishes off that Key all the time. Developing the island would ruin his spot too. He cleans up off that point, sometimes every day for a week or two. Never figured out what he's fishing on. I've been back and forth with a depth finder and can't figure it out. You know if I can get a few beers in him he'll spill his guts. Then I'll decide."

"Well, stay away from scarface there." Roc finished his beer and opened another. He motioned to Will, looking surprised when he accepted. "Wow, two beers. You okay?"

Will ignored the comment but took the beer. "Got a letter from the building department. It says they're not going to renew the permit on my house again."

"And that surprises you? It's been what, five years? You know there's a whole new set of codes now, don't you? That house will never comply with them if you let the permit expire. Maybe we should head over there and see what it's going to take to finally finish that thing and get them off your back."

"Sure, if you don't mind," Will said, dreading what his friends inspection might reveal.

* * *

Fifteen minutes later, they pulled into the gravel driveway. Will got out, opened the gate, and followed Roc's truck in. He looked with fresh eyes at the unfinished house. Left to his own devices, he could live with it like this and it irked him the city was after him again. What was it hurting anyone if he was comfortable here. Every year he went down and wrote a check to renew the permit and every year they took the money — until now.

He followed Roc around the building, trying to guess what the contractor's eyes saw as he inspected the exterior.

"Not too bad. Stucco, lighting, that kind of thing, and you should be okay out here." Will watched Roc's glance as he looked at rough grade surrounding the house. Clumps of grass had started to grow in the mounds of dirt. "It's going to take a little tractor work to get this in shape. You need to have some drainage here.

Maybe a day to fix it, and then they'll make you cover it with gravel or plant it. Let's go see how much trouble you're in on the inside."

Will led the way up the stairs and opened the door. Roc walked in behind him and started walking through the house, clearing his throat as he noticed all the half finished work. "I'm almost done in here," Will said defensively.

"You know, it's close. Finish the bathroom, install counters and a real stove, and they should let you go. I forgot to ask when we were outside, but did you get a final on your septic system?"

"No. It's installed and I had the inspector come out. He gave me a list of a few things to do, but I never called him back."

"Well, you could be in trouble there. That's a separate permit than the house, and if it's expired you're in deep. The old systems are not allowed anymore. If you can even get a permit, it's gonna cost about fifty grand to get the new engineered systems installed."

They finished the inspection and were at the table, each with a fresh beer. Will had a pile of papers spread out in front of him. He offered one to Roc. "This is the original permit."

He waited while Roc looked it over. "This is over five years old. It shows a failed inspection four years ago. You got anything else in that pile?"

Will was almost at the bottom, the documents getting older as he got lower. His filing system was to put everything in a box, new stuff on top. "That's all I've got on the septic permit."

"I got a buddy down at the city. Let me see what I can do for you, but you better be prepared for bad news. Look on the bright side, you finish it right it'll be worth some real money," Roc said.

"Yeah, but you know there's too much of my soul in this to sell. It's just finding the money now that I'm worried about." Will looked out the sliding glass doors to the water, trying to think his way through everything Roc had said and wondering how much money he would have to come up with to finish. He saw a boat idling right on the edge of his property. He squinted at it, trying to see more clearly. "That's the Grady-White. What are they doing here?" He got up and went out on the deck, Roc trailing close behind.

They leaned against the railing and watched the boat. He could see Braken pointing to his house, talking to the another man standing beside him. He pointed again, and the driver started toward his property line. Slowly, the boat approached the mangroves that separated his property from the water, turned and started idling toward the far end of the property.

"They're sizing the place up." He wondered what was going on. First his favorite fishing spot and now his house.

"I'm going to the marina to see if Cody's there. It's a pretty sure thing that if he's not, he'll be at the bar across the street. Need to talk to him about what his dad's up to." He turned toward the door.

"Don't do anything stupid. It's after three, and he's probably had a few. I'll head to City Hall and see what I can do about the permits."

* * *

The dock was empty when he pulled up to the marina. He walked towards the office, bumping into a newspaper machine and then ricocheting into the door, "Hey, Ned, got any cold ones?"

"Yeah, might have a few. Looks like you've had a couple already." The old man stared at his jaw. "What happened there?"

Will ignored the question as he tried to count the beers in his head. "Just a few. Where's Cody at?"

"Should be back anytime." Ned glanced at his watch. "Took a couple of guys out a little before noon."

Will took the cold six pack and went to the picnic table shaded by a small rustic structure built with a palm frond roof and watched the water, his head nodding as the beers took hold. He jumped up when he heard the motor. The boat was running faster than the idle speed limit, as usual, Cody behind the wheel, two clients leaning against the opposite gunwale. Their body language told the story of the day — no fish.

Will walked down to the dock as the boat pulled up and tossed a line to Cody's waiting hand. "Can you give me a minute when you finish up here? Something I need to ask you."

"Yeah, whatever."

Will went back to his table, and Matt walked up to the boat just as the men finished paying Cody. They walked up the dock empty handed, sour looks on their faces. He heard the raised voices and looked back at the boat; Cody was shouting at Matt..

"Where the hell have you been? You're an hour late! What about cleaning the fish and the boat?" Cody yelled.

Matt's voice was barley audible. "Sorry, I had to stay late at school and finish a project. I'll clean the boat."

"Shouldn't be too hard. No fish today." Cody left the dock and walked toward Will. "You're gonna have to buy me a beer if you want to talk. Slow day out there, but I guess you know how that goes."

Will let the comment go and got Cody a beer. He needed information more than a fight right now. Cody grabbed the can before it was offered. He chugged at least half of it, put his finger up for Will to wait, belched and finished it. Will handed him another hoping the pump was primed now, "I saw your dad off Flamingo Key. Looks like he was doing some kind of real estate thing. Any idea what he's up to?"

Cody drank half the second beer and got in Will's face. "Why would I tell you what my dad is doing? Even if I knew." Then Will saw him focus on his face. "What happened there, pretty boy?"

"They ran your boat aground on the back side of Flamingo. I tried to help, but the driver popped me."

Cody laughed. "Just your luck. The old man's got some dude from Miami down. Looking for some land or something. Who cares, as long as he closes the deal."

Now that Will knew Cody knew something he pressed harder, "*I* care. They keep developing the small Keys out here, the fishing's gonna die off. The flats get all silted up and the fish are gone. "

"I ain't worried. I got my spots," Cody said.

"Still can't figure how you do so well off the point out there." Will tried to keep him talking. If he stroked Cody's ego, his mouth would keep going. "Here, want another beer," he set another one on the table without waiting for an answer

Cody stared at him and stopped talking. Will wondered what he'd said to cause this reaction. Suddenly Cody got up and took one beer in each hand. "Sorry, can't help you. But, hey - thanks for the beers."

Matt walked up as Cody was about to walk away, "I'm done. Can I get a ride? I have a ton of homework."

"I got homework too, at the bar. Gonna have to do some damage control to the old reputation after striking out today."

"I'll give you a ride," Will offered. "To your mom's?"

"What's this?" Cody blurted. "First off, you don't need to be taking care of my boy. And second off, you got no business with his mom. You know we're getting back together," he boasted. "The boy can walk." He slammed the empty can on the table and got up to leave.

Will watched Cody walk away, three beers poorer and nothing to show for it. But he also knew no real harm had been done. Cody would probably forget the incident by tomorrow.

"Nah, It's okay - I'll walk," Matt said.

Will watched him walk away, chastising himself for the beers he had drunk, knowing Matt had seen it.

STEVEN BECKER

Chapter 6

Eli Braken sat behind his desk, the ceiling fan doing little to remove the beads of sweat accumulating on his brow. His shoes were off, his stockinged feet set on a desk drawer to try and alleviate some of the swelling he was prone to, mostly from carrying three hundred pounds. On the desk top sat a tumbler with an inch of Scotch next to a computer monitor and a phone. Now past sixty, Eli considered himself hip. He knew how to email and even had the Facebook thing going. He looked past the man sitting in front of him to the logo of The Kraken painted on his wall. The legendary sea monster adopted as his logo after seeing it in the *Pirates of the Caribbean* movies usually brought a smile to his face. He pictured his business as having many powerful tentacles like the monster and had even considered changing his surname.

"Can you put your goddamned shoes on?" The man with the scar sat across the desk, elbows resting on the surface.

"Never mind my shoes. Have you talked to your boss?" He set his feet down and leaned into the desk until his belly hit his thighs.

"Here's the deal. I talked to the guys in Jersey. If that island out there has a sewer and water line that'll service six to eight houses, then they're in. You do have the Army Corp of Engineers okay on the dock too, right?" he asked.

Braken changed the subject. "How are you going to dodge the permit issue? Those bastards in Monroe County passed that Rate of Growth Ordinance in 1992, pretty much shutting down new construction. They only give out about sixty permits a year

34

now. I got my end handled, but your guys will never get ROGO approval to release all those permits. It'll take years."

"Yeah, well people in Miami never heard of a ROGO whatever. It's only sixty miles, but it's a freakin world away from this sandfly-infested pile of coral. We're just selling land, anyway. They know you got water and sewer, they're all in. All those greenies will be waiting in line for solar panels and windmills. A few pictures on the world wide whatever and boom, sold out."

Braken leaned back, satisfied that this deal was going to be easier than he thought. "Your call." He sipped his drink and offered the man a cigar. "Now about that other thing. That guy you punched out on the boat is not going to let this lie. My son, Cody, already had a run in with him at the docks. You want that piece of mangrove-infested sand out there, we need to deal with him now. I've never known him to have a spine, but you never know what'll get someone riled up. And what about the tank?" He was starting to worry about his involvement with Pagliano and the Jersey Mob.

"What? You got cold feet already?" Pagliano smirked.

Braken hid his expression behind the glass of rum. They had done several deals together. When they went as planned they lined his pockets, but a few had gone badly and when they did it was ugly. Not every deal got you rich, he knew, but the Jersey mob had other ideas and the type of damage control that Pagliano was famous for could easily land him in jail.

They hadn't had a big score in several years and he knew Pagliano and his bosses in Jersey were chomping at the bit for this deal to go through. The cost of the Key was nothing compared to the potential revenue when they sold lots. An environmentally sustainable island retreat - a marketer's dream. *If this one could only go well*, he thought.

"I don't get you, Braken." The voice was broken and hoarse. "Back home, we want something, we take it. We just dumped a crap load of chemicals in there today. There won't be any evidence."

"It's a different game here. It's too small a town to make people disappear. I'll bet by tomorrow morning, half the people on this spit of sand will know about our visit to the Key."

"That fishing guide again? Why's he got you all jiggy?" Pagliano relaxed. This was getting into his wheelhouse now. "I suppose you have some ideas about this? After all, it's your neighborhood."

"Actually, I do." Braken finished his drink. "He's got a nice property, but he never got a final on the house. I know from a source at the building department his permit's going to expire. That'll give us some leverage with him. Offer him his permits back if he stays out of our deal."

"And if he doesn't go along?"

"Then we play hardball and have it condemned or whatever they do. I got some connections, and we can buy the property before it goes to auction. We'll make some nice coin on it, and you can do your thing to him."

"Sounds like we're seeing eye to eye here." The man got up to leave. Then he paused and turned. "Just one more thing. I got your boy's gambling debts on hold right now, but if this deal doesn't go through, I'll do 'my thing,' as you say, to collect what he owes."

Braken watched as the man left the office. He realized he had been holding his breath and inhaled.

* * *

Will sat at the table, half a beer growing warm in front of him. He figured it was his sixth — way over his limit. It'd been a long time since he'd been this drunk. Ned had given him the last beer when he locked up a half hour ago. Since then, he'd just been staring at the darkening water, trying to make sense of the day. First the permit thing with the county, then Braken at Flamingo Key, and then casing out his property. It couldn't be a coincidence.

His hate and distrust for the patriarch of the Braken family ran deep, partly because he enabled Cody to prance around like he did, and more for his crooked deals. He'd been a judge just long enough to make all the connections he would ever need, and short enough to avoid any investigations. But what was he up to now? And what could he do about it?

The sound of a car broke him from his thoughts, and he glanced up.

An old Corolla was pulling into the lot, rolled to a stop, and Will watched as a woman got out. He saw her coming toward him, and wished he hadn't had the last five beers.

"Hey, have you seen Matt?" Nicole asked, her face breaking into a smile when she recognized him.

The same feeling returned that he had felt last night, stronger now because of the beer. He tried to compose himself. "He left a while ago. Cody told him to walk home."

"Nice. Where did that son of a bitch ex-husband of mine go? No, let me guess, he's at the bar," she spurted. "Sorry, I didn't mean to dump that on you." She sat down and pulled her phone out, typed in a text message, and set it down. "So, Will? You got a last name?" She leaned towards him.

He hesitated and the phone vibrated. She picked it up and typed a response.

"Well, Will whatever, he's home, no thanks to you." She punched him lightly on the arm.

"Normally I would have driven him, but I've had a few too many of these to drive." He grabbed the beer and held it up.

"Wish my ex would learn that trick." She leaned over toward him again. "Maybe we should get some food in you. Take the edge off."

His mood lightened, "But what about Matt?"

"He's sixteen."

"Sorry, never had kids. That stuff is way above my pay

grade," he said.

"Never mind all that. Let's go." She picked up the beer and finished it, then tossed the can in the trash. "Come on. I'm driving."

He got up slowly, not sure how his legs would react. They worked to his satisfaction, and he followed her to the car, got into the passenger seat and blushed as she smiled at him. She pulled out into traffic, heading South on US1. "How 'bout Keys Fisheries?"

"That'd be good. I guess I could use some food." She turned the radio on to a hip hop station and started bopping to the beat. He watched the storefronts roll by as she drove, trying to avert his eyes as she glanced over at him. As they were about to turn he noticed the sign for Kraken Ventures. "That's your father-in-law's business isn't it?"

"That would be my *ex* father-in-law. Don't care much for that man, or his offspring — the apple doesn't fall far from the tree." She turned right on Thirty-Fifth Street and pulled into the gravel lot. The single-story building housing the market and kitchen was dwarfed by the two-story tiki bar set off to the side in front of the marina. Generally packed during the season, the voices of a few locals were the only sound coming from the raised bar tonight.

They walked past the stairs leading to the tiki bar and went to the order window, halfway down the older building. "I'm going to have a hogfish sandwich, what about you?"

Will realized he hadn't eaten all day "The lobster reuben. I'm starving."

"That'll fill you up." She ordered and paid the cashier before he could offer. "I got it. Just a small thanks for looking out for my boy."

"Next time's on me," he blurted out.

She looked him over and winked. "Okay, you're on."

Sodas in hand they walked over to the rail. Standing close to each other, they looked down at the tarpon swirling around the submerged light. The fish seemed to look up in a Pavlovian response, as most of the tourists fed them.

Will watched and wondered how tonight was going to go. He knew he'd had too much to drink and there was bound to be retribution from Cody when he found out he had gone to dinner with Nicole. But right now he didn't care about anything but the warm body pressing her hip against him. The loudspeaker called out *Natasha,* disrupting his thoughts. Instead of asking for your real name the restaurant asked for your favorite cartoon character. Strange how it usually embarrassed him and he often avoided the place for this reason - like you could feel every eye in the place judging you for your answer.

Nicole returned a minute later with two plates of food. She guided him to an empty picnic table by the water. "Natasha? That's your favorite cartoon character," he asked once they were seated.

"It's nothing, they just make you give a name. Always liked her spirit."

Will eyed the overstuffed Lobster Rueben, knowing it would be better eaten with a knife and fork, but tore into it anyway. The first bite disrupted the equilibrium of the food and half fell onto his plate. Slightly embarrassed he looked at Nicole, thankful that she was engrossed in her own sandwich. He finished what was left in his hand and wiped his face. "Hard to eat," he muttered, and reached for a knife and fork. More conscious of his manners, now, he finished the plate off. He felt better, the food absorbing the alcohol in his stomach. While he watched her eat, his mind drifted back to Braken.

"What's on your mind? It looks like smoke's about to come out of your head," she said, pushing her plate aside.

"It's nothing, just ran into your father-in ... I mean *ex* father —"

She cut him off. "That's a mouthful. I just call him Braken, like everyone else. What's the old creep up to?

"Twice today, I ran into him with some guy with a scar across his head. Once out at Flamingo Key and then again at my house."

"That have anything to do with that lump on your face?"

"Yeah." He told her about the boat grounding and his meeting with Scarface.

"Scarface is Joey Pagliano. You might want to stay clear of him." She paused, "Unfortunately I still work for the old man," she explained. "Don't like it at all, but Cody never pays his child support. I think the old man overpays me to compensate for his son. He's creepy though. You should see the way he and Pagliano look at me. If it wasn't for the money, I'd try and help you, but I can't get by without it."

She picked up their plates and dumped them in the trash. He was about to rise, but she sat down next to him. "Let's forget about the Brakens."

Chapter 7

The sun appeared over the window sill and smacked Will in the face. He rolled over in an attempt to ignore it, but the pounding in his head and the pressure in his bladder forced him out of bed. A quick glance at his watch through fuzzy eyes revealed that it was almost ten a.m. Back from the bathroom and a handful of ibuprofen later, he squinted out the window. *At least the wind was blowing*, he thought. No charters, and no way he was going out on his board in these conditions. Relieved of responsibility, he went back to bed and tried to reconstruct the past twenty-four hours. The last thing he remembered was an awkward kiss at his door. He ran it over and over in his head, more detail emerging each time, but she still left every time and he couldn't remember why. Confused he drifted off.

Voices in the yard woke him. Shaking his head, he tried to clear the cobwebs and listened. He strained to hear what they were saying, but couldn't make out anything. One foot at a time hit the floor, and he was out of bed. And then he sat back down, hoping the room would stop spinning. But the conversation continued, moving closer to the bedroom window. With an effort, he made it to the window and looked at the yard. Two men were standing outside, looking at the house. One was clearly a city inspector; dressed in a uniform shirt and hat — making notes on a clipboard. The other man came around the corner, and Will was relieved to see it was Roc.

"Gimme a minute!" he yelled, his breath ragged, mouth bone dry. He tried to count the number of beers he had yesterday but lost count at around ten — way out of his comfort zone. As he brushed his teeth he tried to remember the last time he had a hangover.

"Sure thing. We'll come up when we're done," Roc called back.

The cold water felt good on his head as he submerged it under the faucet of the laundry sink, temporarily standing in for a bathroom vanity. He would have taken a cold shower, except that the only working shower was outside. The mirror told the tale of the night before, the bottle of Tequila sitting empty on the floor by the bed visible in the reflection. It took another minute to brush out the bed head and put some clothes on.

He was nearly dressed when Roc came in the front door without knocking, the inspector following behind. Will walked out of the bedroom.

"Man, you look like crap," Roc said.

"Yeah, well yesterday wasn't one of my better days." He rubbed his sore jaw.

"This is Bill McLean. He's the building inspector. I talked to him about your permit, and he agreed to take a look with me. See if we could bail you out of this mess."

Will tried to say something, but his mouth was too dry. Instead, he nodded, and the inspector chimed in, saving him the trouble. "We try and take care of the full timers here. It's not like you're some developer from up North."

Will squeaked out a "thank you," and the inspector handed him the clipboard, which held pretty much the same information Roc had told him yesterday. The list wasn't long, but it looked expensive.

"Let me have a look around inside and I'll finish it up. Roc assured me you could have this ready for a final in thirty days. I talked to my boss, and he said we'd give you that. But you've got to get an extension and finish the work on the list."

Relief swept over Will as he handed the clipboard back.

Thirty days was better than he had expected. The way Roc had talked he had figured the extensions were over and the house would be condemned or something. Any way you looked at it this was the best case scenario. As soon as the inspector was out of earshot he turned to Roc, "What about the septic thing?"

"That's all? I pulled some big strings to get this done. I'm working on it, but it's environmental health, not the building department that has to sign off on that."

"Sorry, I'm not thinking straight here. Thanks for doing this."

"You can say that again. Look, get some rest and we'll figure out a plan tomorrow. I still owe you a bunch of work for all the fishing trips."

"Rest is going to be hard to come by. I've got to figure out how to raise the money to do all this."

* * *

Braken had just gone to lunch, leaving Nicole alone in the office. There were almost twenty employees on the roster of Kraken Ventures, mostly part-time Realtors. It was well known in the real estate community that Braken would take in the strays, without looking too closely at whatever they were being investigated for. As long as they still had a license, they were usually welcome. Since it was pre-season now it was slow and most of the Realtors just checked in once a week or so, explaining the empty desks. A few came into the office regularly, and those that did, had coffee, read the newspaper, and left well before lunch. Which meant she had the place to herself, for now.

Her thoughts went to Will and how maybe, she had finally found a nice guy. And he already knew Cody. Most of the other nice ones got one whiff of her ex and took off running. Cody would still be a problem — he always was and Will was a little timid. *That might be a problem*, she thought. Although she hadn't wanted to, Cody was the reason that she had cut short their kiss at his front door last night. It wouldn't hurt her in the long run though. Usually confident with men, after years working bars, she was unsure about Will; whether he was just shy or not that interested. There was a way to put things in her favor.

She took a quick look outside and went to Braken's office, locking the door behind her as she entered. As the office manager, she had a general overview of what happened in the firm, but Braken was notoriously close-mouthed until his deals were done. Then he would bring her in to handle the paperwork. So if he had something big going on, there was a good chance he wouldn't have told her about it.

She moved over to his desk and quickly checked the drawers finding nothing but a bottle of bourbon and a few porno magazines. Behind the desk was a credenza, its surface also bare. A search of those drawers revealed nothing.

Her last chance was his computer. She hit the power switch, thinking it was probably in vain as he password protected his files, and waited while the computer booted up. An idea hit her as she scrolled the file directory with most files showing the symbol of a padlock next to them. If she couldn't see the files, maybe she could figure out what he was up to from his internet searches. He might have been paranoid, but he had no idea about search histories and cookies. She opened the Internet browser, went to the history and scanned through the results. The screen was cluttered with sites, but none of them told her anything important.

She was running out of time before Braken returned. Pulling out her phone, she snapped a picture of the screen. Quickly she turned off the computer and left the office as she had found it.

Back at her desk, she composed herself, breathing deeply to control her racing heart. A few beads of perspiration on her forehead were the only sign that anything out of the ordinary had occurred. The office was empty, and not expecting anyone, she pulled out her phone and stared at the picture on her screen. Using two fingers, she zoomed in on the sites in the browser history. Ignoring the porn sites, she entered the address of what looked like an advertisement on her computer.

She laughed to herself as the site loaded: *Sustainable living in the Florida Keys.*

That was a joke to anyone that knew this area. There was nothing sustainable in the Keys. Food, water, and power were all sent via truck, pipeline, or cable from Miami. So what was he doing researching something like that?

She lifted her head hearing the door open, then quickly looked down and minimized the screen just as Braken and Pagliano entered.

"Any calls, sweetheart?"

She cringed as he said it. "No, it's been quiet."

"Nicole, too bad Joey's got to go back to Miami tonight. You two could maybe hit it off." He winked at the man, then at Nicole. "Maybe next trip." She put on her best fake smile.

The man stared at her as he made his way to Braken's office. On his way out he stopped at her desk and leered, "Yeah, Nicole, maybe next time." He turned to Braken, scowling, "Follow up on that guy's house permit."

"Sure thing, Joey. Nicole, you're on your own, I gotta go to the building department."

The screen reopened the minute they were out the door. Trying to erase Pagliano's leering look from her mind, she scanned through the sales page, her eyes, experienced at searching real estate listings quickly guided her to the fine print.

The site was built by a pro. Slide shows for pictures and search engine terms embedded everywhere, the keywords and meta data geared toward the green movement. It showed a picture of an island with white sand beaches and turquoise water. Next to the picture was an artist rendering of the same island with a cluster of bungalow-style houses sporting solar panels and windmills. A few paragraphs down revealed the cost of investing in the first sustainable community in paradise. A mere $1,000,000 investment got you a share in the golden future. Instantly she knew what they were up to. Flamingo Key had been for sale before and had just been re-listed at a rockbottom price — with the market in the dumps it was cheap. It had infrastructure which made it look attractive on the surface, but anyone knowing Monroe county knew the chances of getting a permit to build there were close to nil. *But*, she thought, *if someone could buy it cheap and sell without disclosing the problems there were millions to be made.*

Anxious to get the information to Will, and hopefully gain some points, she grabbed her purse and headed out the door. Matt would be getting out of school in a few minutes. She could pick him up and see if he knew how to find Will. Otherwise, Ned at the docks was sure to have a number. A quick text to Matt that she was on her way to pick him up and she pulled out of the parking lot and headed towards Sombrero Beach.

Matt was waiting on the sidewalk when she pulled up below the painted dolphin fish; mascot of the Marathon High Dolphins.

"What's up, Mom? You never pick me up."

"You know how to find Will?"

"Jeez, mom aren't you being a little, you know, aggressive?"

"No, it's not like that. I promised I would look into something for him."

"I got his number. You could have just texted me for it." He went to the contacts in his phone and sent her Will's number.

Her phone chimed. "Okay, smart ass. You can walk for that."

"How about a ride to the dock? I got there late yesterday and Dad had a fit."

The Corolla turned right onto Sombrero Beach Road. *Pretty fine real estate for a school*, she thought as she passed the houses lining the road, boats visible in the canals in their back yards. She followed the road to US1 and turned toward Ned's marina, where she dropped Matt off. Once out of sight, she pulled over and hit the number Matt had sent.

"Hello?" The raspy voice was hard to hear.

"Will, is that you? It's Nicole."

"Hey." There was life on the other end, now.

"I've got something you need to look at. You know, what you asked me to do." She took a chance, and barged on. "Why don't you come by for dinner later. About six?" She hoped he would take the bait.

"I thought you said you couldn't," he said.

She had doubted he would remember how the conversation had gone. "Well, you seemed so upset it was the least I could do." Hoping she dodged a bullet she waited.

"Cool. I'll be there."

Chapter 8

Will woke as the sun was about to set, disoriented when he noticed the light was on the wrong side of the house. It took a few minutes to realize that he had just wasted an entire day. He remembered the meeting with Roc and the building inspector earlier, and then the call from Nicole. Panicked, he reached for his phone and saw that it was 6:15. Already fifteen minutes late, he jumped out of bed and showered quickly. A calculated decision that it was worth not being any later than he already was, he waived shaving, looked in the mirror, and brushed his hair. Dressed and out the door, all within ten minutes of waking, he started the truck, opened the gate, and accelerated down the road.

He saw Matt run out the door to meet him just as he pulled into the driveway. "Will, you made it. We were starting to worry about you after yesterday and —"

"Sorry, I got stuck doing something. Where's your mom?"

Matt led the way up the path to the house. The yard was mostly gravel with a few randomly scattered small plants, Nicole was obviously not into landscaping or maintenance. The house needed work, paint was peeling from the railings, and the weather showed it's effect on the old siding. Although he could see a few rust spots, the metal roof seemed to be in serviceable condition.

He rubbed the stubble on his face subconsciously as he waited for Nicole to come to the door. Head down, he felt guilty and empty handed. After a lingering look, it was obvious that she had spent quite a bit more time on grooming than the ten minutes he had. He was startled as she came toward him with a quick embrace.

"Sorry, I'm late, and…" he said holding out his hands.

"It's okay. Come on in."

He could tell from her body language that she was a little tipsy. "Nice place," he said as he entered the living room and walked toward the bar separating the kitchen from the dining area. Two wine glasses sat on the Formica counter; one a quarter full, the other empty alongside a half empty bottle of red wine.

"Go ahead. Help yourself."

He looked at the bottle, not sure if it would help or hurt him. Deciding the chances were good that it couldn't hurt, and not wanting to be rude, he topped off her glass and filled his. "I'm sorry I didn't think to bring anything," he said trying to avert his increasing guilt as she opened the lid of the pot.

She ignored the apology, smiling. "Most guys I know wouldn't even think about it." She changed the subject, "So, I got curious yesterday after what you said the other night. When the old man went for lunch, I was alone in the office. I found some information for you. Braken had a website in his browser history I think you might be interested in." She thrust her breasts forward, stopped and offered him a spoon to taste the sauce.

"Wow, that's great," he said about the touch, the information, and the sauce.

"Let's eat and then I'll show you. Matt!" she called. "Dinner!"

Nicole rattled on about this and that as they ate. Mostly shopping and celebrity gossip about people Will had never heard of. Matt sipped Coke from a can, while Will and Nicole drank wine. Will was famished, realizing that he hadn't eaten all day, and plowed through his first plate of pasta. He looked at Nicole for approval for seconds, and she smiled.

"Sure. It's kind of nice to cook for someone that appreciates it." She glanced at Matt.

Matt took the hint and cleared the table. He left with an

excuse to do homework, leaving Will and Nicole at the sink brushing hips and washing dishes. She smiled at him with every dish he handed her. He wanted to prolong the moment, their bodies touching with each movement, but was also anxious to see what she had found about Braken. "That was a great dinner. Thanks," he said, handing her the last plate.

"Why don't you pour another glass of wine and we can have a look at what I found?"

He poured the remainder of the wine in her glass and brought it to the computer where she sat waiting for the screen to load. Bringing a chair from the table, he set it next to hers. They huddled around her computer desk staring at the screen. "My connection's a little slow here," she said as the page started to appear.

It took only half of the image for Will to recognize the setting. "You've got to be kidding me. That's Flamingo Key." Will said as he read the blurb under the picture. The page was skillfully crafted to show an artist's rendering of the completed community carefully highlighting the environmental amenities. He clicked through to the investors' page. She sat quietly as he read the page. "They're offering unbuildable lots for a million each."

"I read the whole thing before you got here. It says that there is water and sewer already there. From my real estate experience those are the two biggies here," she said.

"Well maybe. But what about building permits. You know the deal here. If it is not a ROGO-approved lot already, they'll have to wait years." He sat back. "They probably bought it for next to nothing."

"I've been working around that office for a long time and seen a lot of foolish people put their money before their brains. They'll look at that picture and be sold before reading the fine print," she said.

Before he could speak, the front door crashed open and Cody entered. Nicole reacted first, moving in front of the computer to hide the screen. Will was slower, but got up, not sure whether to protect her or distance himself.

"What's this little lovefest?" Cody yelled as he stumbled toward them. Matt came out of his room and stood in the hall, uncertain. Cody rounded on him. "This doesn't concern you. Go back in your room. I'll deal with you when I'm done with these two."

Nicole went towards him, "You have no right barging in here. I'm calling the police right now." She held up her phone and hit 911.

Cody ignored the threat, "We may be divorced, but you're still the mother of my boy. That gives me rights." Cody came toward her, but Will stepped between them. "Step aside. It might be best for you if you just split and leave my family alone."

Nicole stepped towards him, "We are not your family. You have no rights here."

As they fought, Will could not help but think that this happened regularly. Their threats and even the way they moved towards each other seemed to be choreographed as if rehearsed. To his surprise Cody swung at Nicole, but missed and landed awkwardly. Will flinched and backed away.

Cody recovered quickly and saw the opening. He charged Will, knocking him off his feet, and they ended up in a ball on the floor. Cody quickly gained the advantage and slammed Will's head on the floor. He was about to slam it again when the sound of a shotgun chambering a round momentarily stopped them.

"Both of you, back away from each other." Matt moved toward Nicole, who was talking on her phone. His hands were shaking, but the barrel pointed at both men.

Will and Cody untangled and separated, neither sure what to do. "Dad, you need to go. The police are on their way and you don't need to be here."

Cody was silent as he got up and moved toward the door.

"This isn't over." He pointed at Will. "Watch your back, and stay away from them." He slammed the door and left.

Matt lowered the gun and went to Nicole, embracing her. "Maybe I ought to go," Will said as he picked himself up. Although adrenaline was pulsing through him, he felt unsure and inadequate at the way he had handled the situation. Nicole had certainly caught his attention and he felt she was interested in him, but he also had a gut feeling it was as much for Matt to have a more stable influence than anything between them. He moved toward the door.

"You don't need to go," Nicole came towards him as he reached the door.

"I'm sorry." Was all he could muster. He went out, closing the door behind him. He turned as he went down the stairs and saw Nicole and Matt looking out the window at him. Unable to face them, he turned toward his truck.

* * *

Will sat alone on his deck. The wind was blowing from the north: a sure sign a cold front was moving in. Stars twinkled above, another indication that the atmosphere was unstable, but he didn't notice. The tequila bottle was in his hand, unopened. His head pounded from the strike to the jaw, the hangover, and from Cody beating it against the floor. He sat there feeling sorry for himself, angry that he hadn't defended Nicole, or even himself. Angry that he had gotten drunk the night before. Angry that he was a spineless piece of crap.

He was having a hard time sorting out his emotions. His self-insulated lifestyle had sheltered him from dealing with the issues he now faced. He was good with boats, fish and wood - not much else and certainly not women. The comfortable life he had built seemed like a house of cards as the problems mounted. His mental image of the purist fly fishing guide, out every day, catching fish with happy customers and then going home to a comfortable house was shattering. One at a time the obstacles were surmountable, but now there were too many and some connected in ways he did not understand. His mind was spinning.

Nicole's affection would have been welcome without the baggage. He already avoided Cody whenever possible. Yeah, he could use some company and he was attracted to her, but as the feeling that she had ulterior motives embedded itself in his mind, the luster was quickly wearing off.

Then Flamingo Key, something he could easily ignore, and probably would if it weren't his favorite flat. Replaying the scene from the other day he recalled the fish bag and buckets on the Grady-White and wondered what Braken and scarface man had been up to.

His monkish existence had served him well for years. *There would be other women and there were plenty of other flats to fish*, he thought as he put Nicole and Flamingo Key aside for the moment.

The house and permits were a bigger issue. Without the means to finish the house he stood to have his permits rescinded and possibly lose the property or at least be forced to move out. That was something worth fighting for, but he didn't know how. He could count on Roc for help, but also knew that he would have to get involved himself. A trip to the building department was probably necessary, something he dreaded; he could deal with fish easier than people.

The only sound was the wind rustling the palm trees as the time passed and his simple solution faded into paranoia. Somehow, he knew this was all connected.

Chapter 9

The wind was blowing twenty knots again when Will woke the next morning; definitely not fishing weather. He checked his email and messages before going out — no charters and with the weather expected to remain the same for a few days it would be quiet. A quick financial calculation put him in conservation mode until Thanksgiving, when the first wave of snowbirds and tourists rolled down US1. With nothing pressing on his schedule, he decided to bike, the preferred method of transport around the island. He pulled the beach cruiser off the hooks in the carport and headed out toward City Hall. The bike path on the northern side of the highway was quiet, the few joggers and walkers waving to him as he cruised by the airport. A right turn on 99th street brought him to the city offices. Sliding the bike into the rack, he locked it, and entered the building.

Cautiously, he approached the receptionist and asked where he could find the building department. Averting his gaze, especially from the city workers, he entered the building department, busy with early morning activity. He took a number and went toward the waiting area feeling like a convict on death row Picking up a two-day-old newspaper, he sat down, and started reading. Halfway through the editorials, he heard his number called.

"Hey," he greeted the clerk, handing her the number.

"How can I help you?"

He looked up at the woman who greeted him with a smile. "I need some help with a permit," he said.

"It's not the dentist here. Lighten up." She smiled. "Got an address or permit number?"

Her eyes were the blue green of shallow water on a clear day and the way she looked at him caused him to stutter, "1557 Eastward Ho Lane. Yeah, I know it's lame."

"Wait here. I'll be back." She winked across the counter.

His eyes followed her until a row of filing cabinets blocked his view. The clerk at the next desk, stereotype of the miserable government worker, must have noticed his interest and shot him a nasty look. He started to count the speckles in the Formica countertop while he waited. Five minutes later she finally came back, carrying two file folders.

"Seems like you've been working on this a long time," she said as the larger folder spilled its contents onto the counter. He already knew that the dates on that paperwork went back the five years since the permit was originally pulled. "It appears you've exceeded the patience of the building official. Last week, the permit was revoked."

"I know, but my contractor brought out an inspector yesterday." He pulled the inspector's business card out of his pocket and handed it to her. "He said that I might be able to get a thirty-day extension." He did his best to smile at her.

"You can petition for it." She handed him a form. "Fill that out and I'll walk it down to the building official for you. The other problem is the waste disposal. Two years ago we went to city sewer. You never paid the connection fee."

"That must have been when they were tearing up the road. So what do I need to do?"

"Go down to the utility department and pay the fee."

"That's it?"

"Well, you could take me to dinner for saving you. Looked like you were ready to jump off a bridge when you walked in here."

He hesitated, after swearing his monkish vows last night, but her eyes intrigued him, "You're on." He was about to leave, but turned back to face her. "Any chance you have one of those files on Flamingo Key?"

She sat up straight and looked at him in surprise, and then over his shoulder, scanning the waiting area. "That's funny. You're the second person this week to ask for that file. Some creepy guy with an up-north accent and a scar on his forehead was in here the day before yesterday asking about it. What's your interest?"

This was starting to get out of his comfort zone, but she smiled again and he dropped his reserve, "Looks like that scar faced guy and Braken are going to try to sell some lots on it," he was surprised by his own voice — almost authoritative. He had taken a chance dropping Braken's name, but got the response he was after.

"Braken? I've had several run-ins with him. Seems like he's always trying to pull some kind of scam. Threatens to go over my head and get me in trouble if I don't cooperate," she thought for a minute. "It's too busy now, but I'll pull it out later and give you a call. You've got me curious what he's up to now." She slid a piece of paper toward him for his phone number.

He scribbled his number and smiled at her, "Thanks," he said as he rubbed his jaw and walked toward the utility counter. Not daring to glance back and break the spell, he stood in line. Suddenly feeling like he needed some air, he went to a wall covered with forms sticking out of plastic holders, took one of each, and walked out.

The image of her smile and eyes the color of the water he loved was all he could think of as he rode. She'd somehow had the ability to calm him rather than unsettle him as Nicole had. Then he smacked the handlebars, how could he be so lame — he didn't even know her name.

* * *

He was back home, sitting at the table, and watching the breeze whip the tall palm trees outside. Anything to distract him from the numbers on the paper in front of him. The total looked to be about $35,000 to finish the house enough to get the final. And it had to be done in thirty days. With an emergency reserve of somewhere south of $20,000, he was considerably short. Even in his best month of chartering, he wasn't going to see $15,000. Will thought about a loan, but with the little verifiable income he showed on his tax return, no bank was going to lend him money.

There was one asset he had that could make that much money — his boat. He hated to compromise his morals and cater to another breed of customer; his reputation was based on catch and release fly fishing, not meat fishing, where the anglers were given every opportunity short of dynamite to load the boat up with fish. But faced with the option of losing the house, no matter how distasteful, he would do whatever was necessary. *Might as well start now*, he thought. Downstairs, he hopped on the old beach cruiser.

The noontime sun beat down on him as he glided down the bike path. He pedaled with resolve and was soon dripping with sweat; the heat and humidity acting like a steam bath, pushing the alcohol through his pours. Gravel crunched under the tires as he skidded into the marina parking lot. Soaked but feeling better, hoping he didn't smell like alcohol, he walked into the office and started to shiver as the cool air hit him.

Ned sat behind the counter reading a newspaper when he walked in. Looking up over his reading glasses he nodded to Will. "Would you look at what the cat drug in."

Will ignored the barb. "Something I wanted to talk to you about. I'm in a bit of a jam, and need some quick cash. The only way I can see getting my hands on it is to do some meat charters for a while."

Ned looked up, staring at him. "Don't look so glum. It ain't like you're going to the dark side — it's just fishing. I can set some up for you, but Cody's going to have a cow."

Will shrugged.

"If you're sure about this, I think I got a charter. Cody offered, but the guys don't really like him." Will took the offered piece of paper with a phone number and stuck it in his pocket.

"I'll just have to deal with him. Did he go out today?"

"No, his charter cancelled because of the weather. I think he's down by his boat."

Will swallowed hard as he left the conditioned air and walked down the dock. Cody was sitting on the transom, spooling line onto a reel, when he walked up. "Hey, I need to talk to you. Seems like I'm short on cash and…"

"Shit, you want to talk to me?" Cody got up and raised his voice. "Stay away from my family and I'll talk to you. Right now, all I got to tell you is to get the hell out of my face."

Will automatically backed away, "I got no interest in Nicole."

Cody jumped up and hopped on the dock. "Don't you walk away from me. Didn't look like that last night," he paused. "See, we're about to get back together you know—"

Will's phone rang, interrupting Cody. He turned away and glanced at the caller ID. *Restricted number* showed in the display. Normally, he wouldn't answer, but anything to avoid a confrontation with Cody.

"Hi, Will? This is Sheryl from the building department."

He started walking away, looking over his shoulder to see if Cody was following. But the other man just stood his ground, scowling. "Hey," he muttered.

"Can you talk?"

"Hold on." He looked over his shoulder again and dropped his eyes when they met Cody's glare. "Did you find out anything?"

There was a pause on the line, and he felt like he was frozen in time, waiting for her to speak. Cody was coming towards him probably paranoid enough to think it was Nicole on the other end. Quickly he said, "If you'd rather get together, we could talk about it later. Maybe get some dinner or something?" He couldn't believe the words had come that easily.

"In person would be better. You have a boat?"

"Yeah, a twenty-one-foot Action Craft flats boat. What do you have in mind?" he relaxed as he looked back and saw Cody leaning against the dock, phone to his ear. *He was probably calling Nicole*, Will thought, *just to make sure she wasn't talking to him.*

"We should take a ride out to Flamingo. There's a hand-drawn map in this file that needs to be verified."

"Sounds like a treasure hunt," he said.

"Not in the way you're thinking. Bring some dive gear if you have it and pick me up at 4:45. I get off at 4:30. That'll give me time to get home and change. I'll text you the address."

"Okay, I'll be there." He disconnected and looked back at Cody.

He was approaching again and Will tensed. Cody started to walk right by him, tossing his usual glare, but that was all. Hoping the situation was diffused and feeling good after talking to Sheryl he blurted, "By the way, just thought I'd let you know that I'm taking some meat charters now." Relieved that he'd confronted him, he waited for a response.

"You? That's a good one. Ain't no skin off my back." Cody laughed, "Those guys need someone to drink with and tell'em jokes. That ain't you, buddy. You'll die a little inside every day." He started to walk away. "Gotta go. Got a date with Nicole tonight."

Will watched him walk away glad that Sheryl had called, glad that he was going to see her and glad that he had taken his vows last night and sworn off Nicole. The turmoil in his head was starting to clear.

Chapter 10

Again, her eyes were the first thing he saw as she walked toward him. If her pupils were fish he would have sworn he was looking into water. He stood motionless as she closed the gap. She was dressed in a tank top, shorts, and flip flops, with a messenger bag slung over her shoulder.

"Ready?" he stuttered.

"Yeah, let's go before it gets dark," she said.

They walked to the boat in silence. Once aboard, he started the engine and tossed the lines onto the dock. Seconds later, the boat was idling out of the canal. As soon as they reached open water, he pushed down on the throttle and the boat quickly planed out. The light hull skimmed across the waves, barely touching some, caressing the tops of others. Will was thankful the seas were down. Earlier today, the ride would have taken more than twice as long as the fifteen minutes it took them to reach Flamingo Key. The boat settled after the wake passed underneath the hull, lifting them, before dispersing its energy onto the beach.

Sheryl had directed him toward the west side of the island. Will looked around, not familiar with this area. He usually fished the mangrove-lined east shore. The tangled root system of the bushes offered cover to the predators waiting for the tide to bring bait fish through the deeper channel running next to the island. This side had a small beach with palm trees.

She took the bag from her shoulder and removed a folder. "This is really interesting," she said as she pulled out a sheet of paper and pointed to a clearing visible in the aerial photo. "It's probably overgrown now, but this Key was partially developed back in the '80s. There are a lot of abandoned projects started without permits and abandoned when they instituted ROGO in 1992. Too much trouble and expense, the Rate of Growth Ordinance shut down all building for a while, especially the homesteaders.

He took the offered papers. There was nothing visible on the aerial photo except the clearing and several paths. The second page was folded in half. When he opened the larger page, it revealed a hand-drawn site plan, which showed the island mostly cleared, with a dock running through the mangroves on the east side and a cluster of small buildings connected by paths that looked wide enough for a golf cart. Two lines were drawn toward the mainland; one marked sewer and the other water. The date was 1988. There was another, older page, also hand drawn, that showed a septic tank and water cistern in a much smaller clearing, with only a single building shown.

"Looks like someone started to permit this as a compound or something, and then bailed on it. They had permits for the septic and water tanks, and apparently finished that, because there was a final inspection." She removed a permit card and handed it to him. "Later, someone else saw a loophole and the upgraded to city sewer and water, thinking it would be easier to get a building permit with the services in place. At that time, there were so many applications coming in that all they looked for was a permitted septic system before issuing a sewer connection. No one noticed that the house had never been built."

"And then it dropped off the radar until a couple days ago?"

"With all the budget cuts we've had, there is no one to check on expired permits, especially the ones out here."

They both turned as a boat pulled up a quarter mile away and dropped anchor. Will squinted at the shape outlined in the setting sun, thinking it looked familiar, and could hear raucous voices as they pulled out fishing poles and started to fish. Someone screamed as they hooked up right away. *Unusual*, he thought; usually you had to set up a chum bag and wait awhile for the fish to find you. Another scream indicated one of the other anglers was hooked up as well. He shook his head and focused on Sheryl.

"Want to go have a look?"

"I would. Some of these Keys have some interesting stories to be told."

He idled the boat closer to the beach, raising the engine as he went. The bow touched sand just as the propeller cleared the water. With the engine off, he went forward and grabbed the anchor line, pulling about twenty feet out. He tossed the anchor onto the beach, pulled the line tight, and looped it around a cleat.

"Unusual way to anchor."

"It's slack tide, and we won't be long. I imagine the mosquitos will eat us alive before we get too far."

She reached into her bag and brought out some repellent, which she quickly rubbed onto her exposed skin. "Want some?"

"Thanks," he took the tube. Both covered in mosquito repellent, they eased over the low gunwale and waded the calf-deep water toward shore. The mosquitos swarmed, but kept their distance as they approached the mangroves. Will went first, clearing a path and holding back branches for Sheryl. He followed what appeared to have at one time been a trail. Forcing their way through the brush, they reached the center of the island and entered the clearing.

He looked around. "There's footprints. Strange, they look fresh. It rained a couple of days ago. Funny, I've never seen anyone come out here; it's all mangroves at high tide and sandbars extend way out at low tide."

She followed him as he moved to the two concrete tank lids, both a foot higher than the sand. "And here're the tanks."

"Wow! That stinks," he said as they approached.

"That's weird. They should be full of water so they don't pop out of the ground when it rains. There's something wrong here."

The image of the large bag on Braken's boat popped into Will's head, and he looked down and followed the footsteps. It looked like there were two sets with the distinct image next to them that the bag would have made if it were dragged through the sand. Emerging on the beach a minute later — the same area that the Grady-White had been stranded on yesterday. Shaking his head, he led her back to one of the tanks. A crowbar lay to the side of the lid.

"This isn't good. Maybe we ought to go back."

"No way. This was my idea." She picked up the crowbar and started to pry at the tank lid.

"You sure?" He watched her struggle for a minute before going over to offer help. She surrendered the bar and he went to work on the lid, walking the crowbar around the opening, the lid rising an inch or two each turn. She came toward him to help as the bottom of the lid became visible, and he handed her the crowbar to hold the heavy lid up while he bent over, grabbed the underside and flipped it.

The stench was overpowering, and he looked into the black void, suspicious of what it was.

"Put it back," she said.

He fought the stench and wrestled the lid back on. They quickly moved to the edge of the clearing, upwind of the tanks. "This is bad. Do you think?" He stopped.

"What?" she asked.

"I had a run-in with Braken and Scarface here the other day. They had one of those fish bags the tournament fishermen use to keep their catch hydrated. It was big enough to hold a man," Will said.

They looked at each other.

"I've seen enough. Let's get out of here," Sheryl said, starting to walk away.

They made their way along the path to the beach, where Will picked up the anchor and carried it back to the boat. Sheryl followed and dove into the water, trying to release the stench from her pores. Back on the boat, they looked at each other, not sure what to do or say.

"Sorry, no towels," was all Will could come up with.

"It's all right, let's get out of here." She started to shiver. "That was creepy."

The boat idled away from the island. "There's a rain jacket in the side compartment. Grab that while I check something out." He watched her wet clothes cling to her body as she bent over to get the jacket.

He looked away as she rose. "See them," He pointed to the fishing boat that was still anchored off the point. It was still loud, rods bent over and fish going in the box. There's no reason for them to be there, no structure just flat bottom, and they're catching fish. It's almost like something is bringing them to that spot. Can I see the map again?" The puzzle was coming together in his mind..

"Sure, but I have no idea what you're talking about," she said.

"Just a hunch," he said, taking the hand drawn map and orienting it. "See, it shows a line coming through there from the water tanks. That was going to be the pipeline feeding the island from the mainland. Let's check it out."

"I don't know Will. I think I've seen enough. Maybe we should just go to the police with this, get cleaned up and then get some dinner."

"It'll just take a minute. Can you grab that spotlight?" He idled the boat around to where he thought the pipe should be and shone the light in the water. "Look, there's a pipe coming out of the sand there." He pointed.

She followed the shape of the pipe, partly buried in the sand, with the spotlight as they moved away from the island and toward the mainland.

The light was fading, the pipeline invisible now, but he followed the direction that they had been heading. Cody's boat was directly in the path of the pipeline and the mainland.

"What the hell, Will. I'm on this spot," Cody yelled as they approached his boat. The other anglers chimed in with him.

"No problem, just having a look around," Will called back not wanting any conflict. He turned the boat and pushed down the throttle.

"We've got limits," Will heard Cody yell to his charter, "What do you say we have some fun."

Chapter 11

The engine noise made conversation difficult as they rode back, each thinking about what they had seen. Will didn't push the boat; ruining his propeller by hitting an object invisible in the dark was not in his budget.

One of the traits that made him a good fishermen was being able to see things that weren't apparent. Most experienced fishermen made the connection between bottom structure and fish, but Will could take it several steps further by envisioning where the fish would hold and at what depth and direction they would be facing at each phase of the tide when they fed. It was also a trait that helped in his carpentry, allowing him to see things in a virgin piece of wood. In his mind he put together the tank, the pipeline and Cody's fishing spot. It would be too much of a coincidence to be anything else. Braken and Scarface were using the tanks to dump bodies and Cody was using the decomposing bodies as chum to attract fish.

Sheryl watched the lights on the shoreline pass by. He liked the fact that she could be close and stay in her own head; unlike Nicole who chatted incessantly. The quiet was broken by the roar of an outboard approaching.

Will looked back and saw the green and red bow lights coming straight toward them. The boat was cruising faster than he was, using the flat water between their wake to gain on them. He figured it was just some drunk tourist, as the boat came close enough to read the registration numbers on its bow before pulling to the side and crashing through their wake.

But it wasn't a drunk tourist. It was the Grady-White with Cody at the wheel bearing down on them.

They watched as Cody and the other men leered at them, laughing as the boat pulled beside them for a second before pulling ahead and cutting them off. The bow of Will's low-riding flats boat crashed through the wake instead of over it, dumping water into the boat.

Will's first reaction was to slow down and let Cody pass by, but he needed to keep speed up to allow the self-bailing cockpit to shed the water. Ahead, the green light shown on the Grady's bow, indicating that Cody had made a turn. The boat roared back at them, running straight toward him until turning again at the last second. This time, Will slowed in time to allow the boat to ride over the wave.

Cody started circling the smaller boat, each circle tightening like a noose, forcing Will to slow further. Waves crashed into each quarter of the boat, soaking Will and Sheryl. Without the forward momentum, the hull would not drain and the boat sank in the water. If he didn't stop they would sink. Will leaned his head over the side to check that the bilge pump was working. A steady stream of water shot from the hull, but he knew it was not enough to keep up with the water the boat was taking on.

"He's going to sink us!" Sheryl screamed.

"I've got an idea. Hang on!"

Will turned the boat toward open water and accelerated. They slammed through several waves created by Cody's boat, taking on even more water, before they broke free of the wake and hit open water. The weight of the ankle-deep water in the cockpit slowed them, but with the boat now up on plane, the water was draining quickly. Will looked over his shoulder and saw Cody turn to follow, and the two boats raced into the night, the faster flats boat gaining a small lead. After a mile, the water, illuminated by the moonlight, subtly changed color. Will continued onto the flat, slowing to turn and watch Cody. He knew that the larger boat would be unable to follow him into the shallow water — if he saw it in time. They watched as the other boat made several passes, staying in the deeper water before turning toward the lights of Marathon.

"What now?" Sheryl was wrapped tight in the rain jacket, but Will could see that she was still shivering.

"He can't get at us in here. The water is too shallow for his boat. Besides, those guys think it was funny now, but he tries anything else, they'll be witnesses."

"No. I mean what now, like in the big picture. He just tried to kill us didn't he?"

Will didn't want to go that far. Cody's attempt may not have been homicidal, but it wasn't a joke either. He wondered if Cody was just out to entertain his charter or if he knew they had found a stash of dead bodies and caught him fishing in the chum slick from them. "Maybe not kill us; more like scare us off."

"Well, it worked." She moved to him.

The embrace came naturally, but ended there. He held her, not sure if she was crying or not, but he was in favor of anything that avoided conversation, so he held on. After what felt like several long minutes, she pulled back and wiped at her eyes, streaking her mascara. "I must look great."

"Actually, you do," he said looking at her as she removed the rain jacket.

She smiled and wiped her eyes with her shirt. "Probably dry better without this."

* * *

They waited an hour, sitting and talking about the island and what had gone on there. Will put out his theory about Braken and Scarface, the fish bag and Cody's fishing spot and why he had been there tonight. Cody fished slack tide. He always came back quickly, with his boat filled. Under normal circumstances, fishermen relied on the moving water created by the tide change to move food and forage. In addition to the tide, they generally used a chum bag, sending scent and small pieces of bait into the current. After twenty minutes or so, fish were attracted to the slick and the real fishing began. But the chum, if you could call it that, coming from the pipeline was best served at slack tide, when Cody knew exactly where it would be. She nodded her head as he spoke.

"Ready?" he asked.

"Yeah, hopefully he's gone now," she said eyes scanning the surrounding water. "We need to decide what to do about this. If you're right and they *are* dumping bodies into the tanks, we need to get the sheriff involved. I'll call environmental health in the morning and tell them about the broken pipe."

"Sounds good. But something is still bothering me."

"There's more?"

"The land scam — why now?" Will put out the untied link.

"The market has come back from its low a few years ago and interest in the sustainable thing they are trying to sell is through the roof. Why not now?"

He nodded, turned the engine on and lifted the pole from the suction of the sand. Slowly he turned the wheel toward shore and started moving off the flat. Once clear of the shallow water, he pushed down on the throttle and headed for the canal entrance, invisible in the dark. Will went slowly hoping that Cody would be in the bar by the time they pulled in, and he could avoid another confrontation. He became more uneasy as they approached the marina. His fears were realized when they pulled within a hundred yards of the dock and heard loud voices. Intoxicated from the beer, their catch, and the chase, the tourists from Cody's charter were sitting on the dock drinking from red solo cups when Will rounded the corner, heading toward his slip. He looked up at the cleaning hut and saw Matt bent over a pile of fish. Cody was nowhere in sight as he tied off the boat.

"I'm freezing. Can I take a rain check on dinner?"

Will was relieved. Maybe he could sneak her off the dock and be out of here before Cody found out that they were back. "I'll catch up to you tomorrow. Maybe I can meet you on your break and we can file a police report. We should do that together."

"That'd be good. I'll call you."

She hopped onto the dock. He watched as she walked away, wondering if she would actually call. After everything that happened in the last few hours he wouldn't blame her if she filed a couple of anonymous reports with the authorities and forgot about him. Maybe that was the best way for him as well. File a report with the police and go to ground until Cody cooled down.

He turned away from watching her as Cody walked quickly toward him, a drunken swagger in his step. Cody weaved past Sheryl, feigning to run into her, but kept going, and she took off in a run toward the parking lot. Will watched the lot, relieved when he saw headlights and a car pull out. Satisfied that she was safe, he turned and faced Cody.

"What the hell was that all about? So I found your fishing spot. It's not like I'm going to steal your numbers or anything." He had decided on the ride in not to let on that they'd found the tanks. Cody had no way of knowing that they had been on the island. In his current state, he might not even realize that they had followed the pipeline to his boat. Will looked at the two men approaching and realized he might have underestimated Cody.

"Dude. If I was worried about you stealing my numbers ... shit," he slurred and moved out of the way as the men approached.

"I gotta smack you again, you're not gonna get up," Scarface said. "You're gonna forget everything you think you might have seen, and lose any interest in that island out there. Understand?"

Will stood speechless, not knowing what to do. Cody must have called them on his way in. Suddenly Matt came up behind the men and interrupted, "Got anything I can do for you? Clean your fish or the boat?"

The men turned to Matt, the heavy one putting an arm around his shoulder and leading him away. Scarface glared at Will again, then turned and followed. Will breathed out thankful that Matt had broken the tension and leaned against the console. He felt something brush against his leg. It was Sheryl's messenger bag. The last thing he needed was for Cody or Scarface to discover the bag and find the map inside. That could make him the next occupant of the tank. He made motions like he was cleaning the boat and stashed the bag in the locking console below the helm. Looking around for an escape, he noticed an adjacent dock light out. He moved toward it quietly, staying in the shadows until he reached the parking lot. Once out of sight, he ran to the bicycle, thankful he didn't need to start an engine, and headed out of the lot.

As he was about to pedal onto the road, a car came barreling toward him. It stopped short, and a head popped out the open window. "Hey, is that you, Will?" Nicole asked.

He pushed the bike toward her, shaking his head. "Not now. I gotta go. Cody's down there drunk again. Sorry," he added as he pushed hard on the pedal, moving the bike into the dark, not waiting for a response. He looked back once he was sure he couldn't be seen and saw Nicole sitting there, head turned toward him. Hoping she'd get the message and move on before he was discovered, he turned and pedaled as fast as the bike would go.

Chapter 12

The men were getting impatient as Will poled the boat toward the flat. He'd gone west today, the opposite direction from Flamingo Key, and the two anglers were drinking their first beers, eager to get their lines in the water when he reached the edge of the hole. This was the first meat charter that Ned had set up for him. Without the GPS numbers most charter captains relied on, he had only his memory.

Catch and release fly fishing, his specialty, was more about tide and covering area, and seldom required anchoring and chumming. He was more adept at reading water and drifting with the current. Over the years, though, a few fixed spots had regularly produced food for his table, and he was heading for one now.

Cody might have been right when he said that a little piece of him would die every time he ran one of these charters.

"We 'bout there yet?" one of the men asked with a deep southern drawl.

"Shortly," Will responded.

"You know there ain't no fish on these flats. I been looking and ain't seen nothing but grass for ten minutes."

"Just about there," Will ignored the comment as he pulled the pole from the water, lifted it high, and set it into the socket to anchor the boat. The water was clear enough to see the bottom from the poling platform and a smile crossed his face as it reminded him of Sheryl's eyes. A jagged edge of grey fell into a darker abyss, indicating depth. Any kind of hole or ledge in the desert of turtle grass and sand held fish. This time of year, as the water cooled, the larger game fish, groupers and snapper, came into the flats and parked themselves in holes and under ledges, where they waited to ambush prey. They'd find fish here, he was sure of it.

He had started early. Having to gear up for meat fishing meant entirely different gear. He had brought half a dozen spinning rods that now sat in the rod holders, their new line glistening in the sun. A quick inventory had revealed that he needed a stop at the bait store to pick up leader, hooks, and sinkers. The woman at the counter was surprised when he asked for eight dozen shrimp.

The pole stuck in the water, acted as an anchor, holding them over the edge of the hole. A scope required with a standard anchor made them hard to use in these shallow waters; the wind and current would often swing the boat away from the hole. There were power sticks for anchors and electric trolling motors that replaced the pole, but the twenty feet of fiberglass was simple and he preferred simple. He had set the boat up current of the hole, and now set a chum bag to drift from the stern. His position would allow the chum slick to drift over the ten-foot-wide hole, tempting the fish to start feeding. Spinning rods were handed to the anglers, shrimp nestled on the hooks. The men followed his directions and cast toward the hole, allowing the small split-shot sinkers to submerge the bait. Then they waited.

He mechanically unhooked fish and rebaited hooks as the anglers worked quickly toward their limit. They fell into a routine and he started to think about last night. Sheryl — her eyes, her body as her wet clothes clung to it, as well as her personality had captivated him and he couldn't stop thinking about her. A quick look assured him the clients were all good and he picked up his phone and went to the recent call screen. He copied her number into the message app and texted her.

* * *

Sheryl glanced around the waiting room. Concentrating on

the customer in front of her was impossible. The chances that anyone would ask for the missing files were remote, but still weighed on her mind, the messenger bag with the file was somewhere on Will's boat. Scarface might come back at any time, and she was nervous She was sure he was the same man that had come into the building department the other day asking for the Flamingo Key file. What if he came in and asked again?

Tapping her pen on the desk, she tried to guide the couple in front of her through the tenuous procedure for a permit. Thankfully, she did this many times a day, and could operate on auto-pilot. They were just wrapping up when her phone buzzed with a text. Her heart started racing, and she grabbed the phone.

Can you meet later? On a charter now. The sender was Will, and she smiled. After too many cocky, arrogant men, she kind of liked his cool, laid-back style. He had handled what could have turned out to be a deadly situation last night with confidence — something she really liked in a man. It felt like they had known each other longer than a day after sharing the experience. She answered, *Need my bag - it's got the file. Yes, let me know when you get back.* Relieved that he had contacted her, she turned back to the application and couple in front of her.

* * *

Matt sat in front of the monitor in the school library with a small group gathered around him. His YouTube account stared back at them, the reflection in the screen showed his jaw drop and the startled look on his face. He had overheard his mom and Will talking the other night, and, unable to sleep, had started researching Flamingo Key. Although not in the conservation club at school, he had strong feelings about the preservation of the Keys. He did his best to hide his disgust for his father's meat fishing business, especially when he brought in undersized fish. Like many teenagers brought up in the Keys, he knew fishing was a way of life, and conservation rather than preservation was the more practical way to save the fishery and the jobs that came with it.

Then there was his grandfather. He knew his mom put up with him because she needed the work, but he was seriously creepy. His permanent distaste for the man was cemented by the offhand comments he overheard from strangers, not intended for his ears, about *that* man being his grandfather. Often embarrassed he wished he was not related to him. A favorite fantasy was that one of the nylon leisure suits he wore would auto-ignite from the sun. Now that would be a cool YouTube video.

Will had taken him to fish Flamingo Key before, taught him about the flies he used, and how to fish them. He couldn't see himself fishing that same flat with the artist's rendering of a village on the island. Green, sustainable or not, he had decided that Flamingo Key should stay as it was, and his tool to keep it that way was the Internet.

It had only taken a few hours to put together a video, cutting and pasting the images from the website, showing the way the island was now, and what was proposed, and with an artistic flair, he showed fish dancing on the pristine water surrounding the island with a time lapse of the development; one by one, the fish keeled over and disappeared. A few keywords and social media posts later, and the video started getting hits.

Now, a day and a half later, it was in seven figures. Over a million hits and growing. It had gone viral.

* * *

Braken stared at the video playing on the screen of his computer.

"One of my people saw this. Look at this shit, over a million views already. This Internet is crazy," Pagliano said.

"And, not good for business," Braken responded. "We need

to get this thing removed."

"It's not so easy. I've got a hacker buddy I know working on it, but it may take some time. We've got to either break into the account of whoever posted this or find them and have them take it off. I'm leaning to the personal option, myself."

Braken looked away from the screen. "I can't watch it anymore. You know what's going to happen if one of those do-gooder groups gets a hold of this? They'll start a protest or something, right out there. Alert the media and all that. Then somebody's going to take a nature hike out there and discover the tanks — we're done. It won't take them long to put our names to it and we'll be in jail. We can't allow this to go any further." He picked up his phone. "I'm going to set up some security out there. Make sure no one sets foot on that sand pile."

"Good idea. I'll keep working my end."

Braken pushed a button on the phone. "Nicole, could you come in here?"

She entered a minute later, steering to the opposite side of the desk from the leering Pagliano.

"We get any inquiries on the Flamingo Key site?" Braken asked.

"Got a couple the other day," she said.

He looked over at Pagliano staring at her, watching her face as she focused on the screen. "What do you have Matt's YouTube page up for?"

They both stared at her. Pagliano was about to rise, but Braken held a hand out. "What did you say?"

"That's Matt's page you're looking at. MattyB97, that's his username."

"Don't you monitor what your son does?" Pagliano yelled. "This is a direct attack on our business venture!"

Braken looked at Nicole, deciding on a softer approach. "You have any idea what Matt's done? Here, look at this." He faced the screen toward her and pushed play, then watched her face as the video played. "You need to get him to pull this, or whatever they do."

She wasn't sure what they were so upset about. "I'll talk to him after school. I don't see what the big deal is, though. It's kind of funny."

Braken sat back in his chair and looked at his partner. Pagliano would show no quarter to his family. The best way to protect Matt was to be hard on Nicole. She wouldn't understand, but it didn't matter. "This can have serious repercussions on our business, Nicole, and that means your job. Do I make myself clear? It needs to go *now*. Not after school. Go find him and take care of it," he said looking at Pagliano for approval.

Red-faced, she left the room. "Well, that was a lucky break. I'm going to keep an eye on her just in case." Pagliano said..

"Yeah, well just an eye. Lay off her, she's family."

Chapter 13

Pagliano followed Nicole. She left the office and drove to the high school. So far, so good. If she did what Braken asked and her boy took down the video, she would never know he was there. Never one to skimp on homework, he'd accumulated enough information on everyone associated with Braken and his family to know everywhere she and Matt went.

He and Braken had been involved in several deals since the early 1990's, but if his partners weren't from his neighborhood in Jersey, he didn't trust them. He stayed at least a block or two back and slowed further as she approached the high school. She must have texted the kid to let him know she was coming, because he was standing outside the school, pacing back and forth. He knew the look of someone who knew he was in trouble, and smirked.

He watched as Matt got into the car. They sat there, the discussion clearly getting more agitated as the minutes passed. Joey knew from personal experience how obstinate teenage boys could be, and wasn't surprised when Matt got out of the car and slammed the door. Before he could walk away, Nicole got out and went toward him. She tried to grab him, but he easily shrugged her off. They stood there arguing, and Joey knew from Matt's body language that he was not going to give in. He needed to add his presence to the situation, to enforce his will.

He pulled up and parked behind Nicole, leaving the engine running and door open as he got out and went toward them. Both turned in recognition, and Nicole's maternal instincts overrode her anger. She moved to protect Matt.

Too bad it was the tropics, or he would have had a gun in his waistband. He wouldn't even need to draw it, just show the outline of cold steel behind the cloth of the jacket, but in eighty degrees you looked pretty stupid wearing a jacket. And drawing the small 22 caliber gun from its holster against his calf would be too visible to any onlookers. Instead, he casually walked toward them, both hands in his pants pockets, trying not to appear threatening.

"Maybe we should take a ride, you know, the three of us," he said to Nicole.

She shied away and Matt puffed up bravely. "What do you want with us?"

"We just need to have a talk, is all. Make sure you all have your priorities straight," Pagliano said.

"And what if we refuse?" Nicole asked.

"You won't. Nobody ever does - and you know it." he said as he put a hand on her shoulder.

She pushed back setting him slightly off balance, "Run!"

Matt took the opportunity and ran towards the protection of the school.

"Damned kid," He pushed her, "Now, let's take a walk back to my car, nice and quiet. Nobody gets hurt." She went to the passenger side, but he motioned for her to drive.

Pagliano looked at the school and then at Nicole. Matt may be gone, but he still had plenty of leverage. He watched the rise and fall of her low cut blouse, her breath coming in big gulps and started to get excited.

* * *

"Sheryl, got a minute?"

She looked up anxiously as her boss hovered over her. "Sure. You're place or mine?" she countered with their usual line. Usually she got a grin, but his face remained neutral.

"Let's go back to my office. There's something you need to see."

She followed him past several work stations to a glass-fronted office. Even the big dogs got no privacy here.

He went to the desk and hit several keys on his computer. "Come around here and watch this."

She moved around the desk and watched the screen. The dancing fish made her smile, but only until she saw the banner on the bottom of the screen. "Yeah?"

"It's Flamingo Key. This thing got on YouTube yesterday, and now it's gone viral. There's over a million hits now."

Her breath caught and she tried to remain calm, "Okay, but what's that got to do with us?"

"I went to pull the file, you know, just out of curiosity about where this kid might have got this, and it's not there." He looked at her, waiting, "You were the last one to check it out. Twice this week."

She looked up at the ceiling, and then down at her hands as she told him about the inquiries from the scar-faced man and then Will. "It must still be at my desk," she got up, "Gimme a few. I'll be right back."

Without waiting for a response she left his office. It took all the willpower she had not to run out of the building, but she controlled herself. At her desk she moved some files around while she thought. There was no way she could have told him where the file was. Best case, it would put a large black mark on her record; worst case it would cost her job. But now, caught in a lie, she needed to get out of here and think. She told the clerk at the next desk that she was going to lunch, got up and went for the door.

Despite the early afternoon heat, she walked. She went out 99th Street and crossed US 1, then turned left on the Heritage trail, a bike and jogging path that ran parallel with the highway. Even staying to the shade she started sweating, but the exercise helped her think.

Will had intrigued her, maybe more than that, she admitted

to herself. There might even be some boyfriend potential there. She just hoped the action on their first date was not a window into his life. It didn't seem that way, and she tried to separate the Flamingo Key situation from him personally in her mind.

Checking her watch she realized that half her lunch was gone and she turned around. Still no text back from Will, but she knew he had a charter and might be out of range. It wasn't lost on her that she was becoming protective, making excuses in her mind for him already. Now she just had to figure a way to stall her boss for a couple of hours and get the file back.

A long line waiting for help greeted her when she entered the air-conditioned office twenty minutes later. She made a quick detour to the ladies' room to freshen up and then went for her desk. Usually dreading this kind of line, she was thankful today. Waiting made the customers cranky and they usually took out their frustrations about the permit process and burdensome regulations on her. But today it was the perfect excuse to dodge her boss.

* * *

Will's boat turned the corner into the basin, the two anglers aboard talking loudly and toasting each other with their beers. Will looked toward the seawall and saw Cody's Grady-White. His heart went still and he looked anxiously around, hoping Cody had finished early and was on his usual barstool next door. When he was sure no one was there, he steered toward his slip and saw Matt pedaling hard down the driveway. Matt must have seen him because he hopped off his bike and ran to the dock. The boy stood waiting as the boat coasted to a stop and he tossed Will the dock lines.

"I've got some fish to clean if you want to make a few bucks. My boys here did pretty well on the snapper," Will called.

Matt shook his head, his face pale. "I really need to talk to you first. Give me a minute and I'll help you out."

Will turned toward the two men. "Why don't you guys go up and have a few beers at the bar across the street? I'll bring your fillets over as soon as I clean up. We can settle up then." He watched the men walk away. When they were out of earshot, he went to Matt. "What's up?" He didn't really want an answer after the revelations about the Braken clan in the last few days. As much as he liked Matt, he was still a Braken. Whatever it was, it couldn't be good.

"That scar-faced dude ... he's got Mom." Matt was almost in tears.

"Slow down and tell me what happened." Will moved toward the boy, hoping to calm him.

Matt paced back and forth, clearly upset, as he told the story.

"If you think this is all about a YouTube video? Why didn't you just take it down?" Will asked.

"I thought she was overreacting. You know, like mothers do. I had no idea —"

"He hasn't called you?"

Matt looked at his phone and shook his head. "Nothing."

"Okay, slow it down. He wants the video down and you want your mom back safe. You've watched enough TV to know how this is going to play out. First he'll get somewhere safe, then he'll contact you. We just have to make something work so you can take down the video and you know he releases her," Will said, trying to figure a scenario that might work in Matt's favor.

Matt was still pacing, turning his back so Will couldn't see his face.

"Maybe we ought to stay together. There's nothing we can do until he calls." Will said, trying to comfort him. He went back to the boat and pulled the fish box out from underneath the leaning post. With a grunt, he lifted it on the dock. "Let's clean these real quick and maybe he'll have called by then. We can figure out an exchange scenario while we do it. It helps to stay busy."

Matt went for the cooler and opened the lid. "Damned nice fish, Will. What's up with you taking so many?"

"Got some money problems I've got to sort out. Come on." They each grabbed a handle and headed for the cleaning table. Once there, they worked in silence, "Slow down, Matt, destroying the meat is not going to get her back." He was filled with as much anxiety as Matt, but tried to work slowly and methodically as they filleted and bagged the catch.

Matt checked his phone again while Will hosed down the table. Just as they were about to walk away, Cody pulled into the lot. "Crap, let me grab something off the boat and let's get out of here," Will said. He ran toward the boat, hopped onto the deck, and retrieved Sheryl's bag from the compartment. He slung it over his shoulder and ran back toward Matt. Too late, Cody was standing there eyeing the catch.

"What's this, then? You been on my spot?"

"Wouldn't go near that place. I got my own numbers."

Cody turned to Matt. "Hear that? Fly fishing dude's got his own numbers." He turned to Will, and eyed Sheryl's bag. "Nice bag. Listen, catch and release boy, we gotta talk about last night. I maybe had a few beers and a rowdy charter. Didn't mean you no harm."

"Sure, Cody," Will said as he tried to move past him. "No harm, no foul." He grabbed the fish off the table and went to his truck, relieved that Cody had been so easy. His concern for Matt had his Cody radar offline; he didn't realize it had been too easy. He started to walk toward the bar, fillets in a bucket at his side, ready to hand them over and collect for the charter.

Chapter 14

Nicole was balled up in the corner of Braken's office. Her top was off and bra torn. Pagliano leered over her, the look in his eyes clearly threatening more if she did not comply. She knew what he wanted — there was only one thing left. Matt had already responded that he would take the video down and they had both watched as it disappeared from YouTube. She had turned to leave, her freedom on the other side of the office door, but he stopped her.

"I got no assurance that he won't post it again after he knows you're safe. See, back in the day, there were real pictures with negatives. Once you had those, it was money in the bank. These days, with the Internet this and that, you never know. I think me and you are gonna spend some time together."

That's when the assault started. She searched for safety, finding it temporarily in the corner, crammed in the small space between the couch and bookcase.. He seemed satisfied for the moment, talking on his phone, assuring someone that everything was under control.

The feeling she had was that everything being under control was her never seeing Matt again.

That realization steeled her. The only escape would be through the door. The office was a second-story space with parking below. At least a twelve-foot drop from the window, if she could even make it out. Who knew when the windows had last been opened, Braken was an air conditioning fiend. The door was at least twenty feet across the room. He'd catch her before she got there. Her only hope was to stay where she was and pray for a miracle.

Unfortunately, she had been here before. Cody had been a mean drunk, and abused her several times before she finally left him. Pagliano had been around Braken long enough for her to know that people disappeared if they met his displeasure. If she were going to die there was no way she was going easily.

"Get out of that hole, would ya? I didn't mean to startle you."

"Yeah, right. I'm good here." She squeezed her knees to her chest.

He went towards her and grabbed her hair; the only part of her he could get at. She screamed as he yanked it and pulled her to her feet. He slapped her once and was in the middle of his windup when the door opened.

"What the hell's going on in here?" Braken stood in the doorway.

"Get me away from this maniac!" Nicole screamed. "Matt took down the video like he wanted. He promised to let me go, and now look!" She held her head up so he could see the bruises already forming. She watched him waver; face red, seersucker pants shimmering as his legs shook.

"Come ,on Joey," he pleaded. "The girl did what you wanted. You need to let her go."

Pagliano turned and pushed Nicole to the couch. "You talkin' to me?" It wasn't a question. "I think a little more respect is in order."

"Say something, you spineless coward," Nicole yelled at Braken as she curled into a ball to protect herself.

"This one over here," Pagliano pointed at Nicole, his face red, "she's trouble. Me and you gonna go take her on a boat ride. Feed some fish, you know." He was moving around like a cornered animal, ready to attack.

Braken shied away. "No way. You've gone too far this time. I've gone along with some of your over-the-top solutions in the past but not this time. She is the mother of my grandchild," he pleaded. "I will —"

"You will do as I say. She's right about the spineless coward thing." He reached down and pulled a small pistol from an ankle holster. "Now, do we have a problem?"

"No, sir," Braken slumped and moved towards the door.

"Go check if anyone is out there. I'll be a few paces behind you." He looked at Nicole. "Cause any trouble — anything, and I'll drop you right here. You'll never see that boy of yours again."

Her blouse retrieved from the floor, she did the best she could to cover herself. Getting shot was not an option. She was going to need to find another way out of this.

As she crossed the threshold her phone vibrated in her back pocket.

* * *

Matt barreled into Will nearly knocking him over as he was leaving the bar.

"He says if I take it down he'll release my mom!" he yelled even though they were practically on top of each other.

"Hold on," Will needed to calm him down, " We've got to stay with the plan. If you just take it down he might not keep his end of the deal."

"I don't care. I'm going to do it right now." His thumbs flew across the screen of his phone.

"Hold on." He had to calm the boy down. His cell phone vibrated and he reached in his pocket and withdrew the phone, *Need the bag, now!* Read the display *Bring it to building department.*

Will put the phone back in his pocket and watched over Matt's shoulder as he opened the YouTube app on his phone and logged in. They leaned against the truck, using it to shade the screen. He watched as Matt deleted the video. "Okay, now text her and let her know."

Matt typed in the message and hit send. "Two million hits. Damn."

"As long as he releases her, it's all good. Someone with some influence may have seen it, and will stop them from developing the island." Suddenly he remembered the text from Sheryl and got in the truck. "Come on. I have to meet someone. Maybe we can pick up your mom on the way."

Matt didn't take his eyes off his phone during the ride to the Building Department. Will felt badly, but was starting to realize how bad Pagliano was — at least a level ten psychopath.

"Don't worry, Matt, he'll call," He tried to reassure him as they pulled into the parking lot of the building department. It was hard to believe just yesterday he had first met Sheryl. "Wait here. As soon as she calls, get me if I'm not back and we'll go get her."

He got through the door just as they were locking up with an urgent plea to see Sheryl. Will took the bag and went inside. Just before he lost sight of the parking lot he looked over his shoulder at Matt, sitting in the passenger seat, oblivious of the heat, head down staring at the phone.

Two customers remained at Sheryl's desk when he walked in. He sat in the closest chair and waited, watching her as she worked. The couple finished their business and he almost ran into them in his rush to get to her, "Here you go. Sorry it took so long. I was out with a charter, and didn't get your text until I got back," he blurted.

"Easy. No problem." She smiled and reached for the bag. "My boss saw that I logged the files out. Now he's all hot, but this ought to settle him down." She tapped the bag.

"Don't you think we should tell him about what we found? Somebody has to do something."

She thought for a moment. "He's not exactly Mr. Action, but he'll listen, and maybe know what to do. Alright."

Will turned away.

"Where are you going? I'm not going in there alone."

Reluctantly, he followed her as they went deep into the maze of cubicles and offices. Stopping in front of the glass-fronted office, Sheryl tapped lightly on the door. The man looked up and signaled for them to enter. He stood and shook Will's hand. "About time Sheryl's got a boyfriend. Name's Adams, Bill Adams."

Sheryl looked wounded by his comment. She handed him the file. "Here it is. I think we should tell you that we went out there and had a look around."

Will watched as Bill's head bobbed, more of a tick than a nod as Sheryl spoke. At the point in the story where they saw the tanks, he got the feeling that this was not the guy to be telling this to. His brow was starting to furrow as she spoke and nothing had even happened yet. It was evident from his face and body language that he was the epitome of a midlevel bureaucrat. This was not someone who was going to help. He tapped her shoulder and stopped her. Apparently she had the same feeling or read his mind as she quickly stopped.

"That's quite a story." He picked up the phone and dialed a number.

"Who are you calling?" Sheryl asked.

He looked sternly at them. "I'm calling the sheriff. You stole a file and trespassed on private property. This looks bad — like you were working for us. I have to do this to clear the department. They'll deal with you, and by the way, you're fired for stealing the files."

She stood. "You piece of crap. I'll bring you up on sexual harassment charges for all your little innuendoes. Come on," she muttered, grabbing her bag. "Let's get out of here."

Will followed her out the door, almost at a run. "Where are you parked? What about the police? He said he was going to call the sheriff," Will said as they reached her car.

"I don't know what to do," she reached for him.

He hugged her, "The best thing we can do is go to the sheriff and report it ourselves before he calls. The office is five minutes away."

Matt was walking towards them, "I haven't heard anything. Maybe we should go to the police."

"That's what we were just saying," Will said as he kept an arm around Sheryl's shoulder and guided her to his truck. The last thing he wanted to do was to lay this mess out in front of an officer, but what else was he going to do.

Chapter 15

Pagliano pushed Nicole into the backseat, then got in next to her. She huddled against the door trying to put some space between them, but he still felt too close. A quick glance at the handle revealed that the door was unlocked. She thought about getting out right now, and started to make a move for the handle, but he was faster and reached across her, rubbing against her breast as he locked the door.

"Try anything stupid, and I'll knock your sweet ass out." He turned to Braken. "Hit the childproof lock thing. I don't want to lose her."

The automatic locks clicked, sealing her in. She knew from raising Matt that the windows would not work either. A solid wall on one side and the leering gangster on the other. She started to cry.

Braken pulled onto the road. "Where to?"

"The marina, you idiot. Find that worthless son of yours. We need his boat."

Braken lifted his phone to his ear, waiting for Cody to answer. "He's not answering. I'll text him."

"We don't need him. This time of day he's probably in some bar drinking. Worthless shit. You got another key for the boat?" Pagliano was getting impatient.

"The old man that runs the place probably has one." Braken said as he turned off US 1.

With every passing minute Nicole knew her chances of staying alive were slipping away. She desperately sought escape, but with a locked door and Pagliano next to her, she would have to wait until they got out of the car before she could do anything. She hoped Will might be around and be able to help. Time was getting shorter as Braken pulled into the gravel lot and parked under a shade tree.

"I'll stay here with this one." Pagliano grinned at Nicole. "Go get the key and start up the boat. Send me a text when you're ready for us."

Nicole watched as Braken got out, leaving her alone with Pagliano. As soon as Braken was out of sight he leaned closer and started to fondle her. With nothing to lose she lashed out with an elbow, catching him in the nose. Blood started to trickle down his face.

"Now, now. Is that any way to treat Uncle Joey?" He slapped her and grabbed her by the chin making her focus on him, "Listen good, because the life of your son is on the line here. You are going to get out of the car and walk nicely to the boat. You are going to get on the boat and sit down. You are not going to start any shit, or your son is dead."

She stared at him a look he knew well on her face — submission.

"Do you understand me?"

She nodded her head, but a sense of urgency flowed through her. There had to be a way out of this and it had to be right now. Once they were on the water she could bail out of the boat if he didn't tie her down — but then what. The thought of floating around in the gulf didn't warm her, but it could be a last resort. Pagliano's phone dinged, interrupting her thought.

"Okay, here we go. Remember what I said."

He got out of the car first and went around to her side. She got out on her own and started walking next to him towards the dock. Her phone vibrated in her back pocket again. Taking a chance, hoping it was a call and not a text, she moved her hand around and slowly lifted the phone out of the pocket. With the same hand she found the round button on the bottom and swiped the screen, hoping to activate the call. The phone slid back in her pocket and she turned quickly to Pagliano. "Where are you taking me? You know I'll cooperate now that you've threatened Matt."

"Shut up, bitch." He reached over and grabbed her butt. "What the fuck?" he pulled the phone from her pocket, wound up and tossed it into the water.

* * *

They stood at the counter of the sheriff's station, a deputy in front of them, taking notes on a form. Will was answering his questions, as patiently as his distaste for authority allowed.

Matt fidgeted and thought, *Why don't they find her now and do the paperwork later?* He looked out the window and saw the streetlights flicker on. It would be full on dark soon, making it that much harder to find her. And still Will and Sheryl just stood there answering questions. They needed to do something, his mom was in danger!

"Just for the record, why don't you try and call her again?" the deputy asked.

Matt set the phone on the counter, put it on speaker, and dialed. He was about to grab it and disconnect when the ringing stopped. They listened intently, Sheryl having to put a hand over Matt's mouth to keep him from talking. The deputy got the idea and reached over to hit the mute button, just as the man told Nicole to shut up. The line remained open, but they could talk freely now.

"You see. They've got her," Matt said.

The deputy reached for his phone and made two quick calls, one to the sheriff and the other to the tech assistant. He turned to Matt. "I'm going to need that phone," he said, grabbing it off the counter. Just as Matt was about to protest losing the only link to his mother, the door behind the counter opened.

"What's up?" the girl asked, looking at the three figures huddled in front of the counter. "Hey, Matt."

He blushed. "Hey, Justine. I didn't know you worked here."

"Got an intern gig. Pretty cool, huh."

"This is your tech guy? She's still in high school," Will muttered.

The deputy looked at him. "Don't you worry. This is right up her alley." He turned to Justine. "Glad you're still here. We've got an abduction. See if you can get us a location on the phone that just called this one."

Matt watched as Justine took the phone and went back through the door. Marathon High School was small enough that everyone knew everyone else - his class was only a hundred. Matt was liked but not popular. His father was a known drunk and his grandfather making the front page of the newspaper too many times, for not the right reasons meant he was often ostracized. Justine's parents had been clear that she stay away from him when he had asked her out last year. In some ways he wished that she had just told him she wasn't that interested or something; anything than it was because of his family. Now he felt awkward whenever he was around her - like he was being judged.

"What now?" Will asked the deputy.

"Why don't you have a seat? The sheriff's on her way." He started shuffling papers, making a noise with his lips every time he wrote.

Will and Sheryl went to the chairs against the wall and sat, but Matt was too nervous. "Hey," he said to Will, "I'll be outside. I need some fresh air."

Without waiting for an answer, he pushed the door open and stepped into the hot evening. He leaned against the building to think. There was something about the phone call that had caught his attention. Adrenaline was running through him and he had to do something.

* * *

The video was gone. Doug stood across from the group and tried the YouTube address again, with the same result. He was slightly embarrassed, but he knew what he had seen, and addressed the group with confidence. The Meetup group consisted of almost a hundred members throughout the Keys, although only a handful had answered his call, probably because of the short notice. He knew that once they had decided on a plan, he would get the support of the entire group — and then some. Development of the out islands in the Keys was a hot topic, and one that environmentalists got passionate about. There was no reason to develop these pristine islands. The impact on the environment from construction and then habitation, no matter how sustainable, was unacceptable to the radicals assembled in front of him.

"Dave, you saw it. Anyone else?"

Four hands went up, giving him enough authority to continue. "It was clearly Flamingo Key. You can tell from the shot showing the mainland in the background. I called the building department and big surprise, the file was missing. I've got a call into the building official, but it's after five on Friday, now. We won't hear back from them until Monday. I say we take action tomorrow while this is still hot. Millions of people saw that video. If I can just find one of them that downloaded it or has it cached on their computer it would help, but even without it, we can act."

The call to action was greeted with murmurs of approval from the group. These were the hard core planners that would drop everything and come to a meeting on an hour's notice. The people who got things done.

"We should send a message for a Meetup to all our members — both the environmental community group and the kayak group. That's at least a couple of hundred people. Tomorrow morning, we meet at the boat ramp by 54th Street and paddle out to the island.

We can form a ring around it and hang out for a while. If we can turn out some numbers, we'll have video and pictures flood Facebook and Twitter. Half the country will know about this by noon.

Doug looked at the group. The excitement was palpable as each member focused on their cell phones and started pecking away invitations and postings. He smiled and thought how easy activism had gotten in the social media age.

In the meantime, his own thumbs flew along the keyboard of his phone, posting to every site he belonged to.

Chapter 16

Braken pulled the phone from his pocket and quickly shut off the sound.

It was too late, though; Joey turned to him, having heard the ring. "Nice ring tone. *Wild Thing*? What the fuck?"

"Oh, that's nothing."

"Do you even know what you're doing with that thing?"

"Kind of. Got some apps, you know, the Facebook, Meetup … keeps me connected."

"What the hell do you have to be connected to? All's you need to do is front my deals, sit back, watch porn and drink Mai - Tais." He reached for the phone. "Let me see that."

Pagliano grabbed the phone and waved it in front of Braken's face to taunt him. He unlocked the screen and opened the notifications window. "What's this? The Keys Kayak Meetup group. Somehow I don't see your fat ass in a kayak."

"Good way to meet the ladies."

He opened the Facebook app to the page, "Shit. That freakin' kid of yours." He pushed Nicole forward, knocking her to the dock. "That video he made has done irreparable damage. There's some activist group posting about some kind of protest out at the island in the morning. This is bad." He grabbed Nicole by the hair and pulled her up. "We need a place to go for the night. Somewhere where the two of you can sit tight while I figure out how to handle this."

"We can use my place," Braken volunteered.

"Think you can handle wild thing here? Or do I have to take care of her now?"

"No, no. I can take care of this." Braken looked around. He had been coerced into helping bring bodies to the tank on Flamingo Key, and even though he had never seen the bodies, he knew he was in deep — deep enough for jail time. Business was business in his mind and no matter the shade of the deal he maintained a clear conscience, but now, he was worried Pagliano's behavior was about to hurt his family. He glanced at Nicole, and knew the damage was already done. "Maybe we ought to get out of here now before anyone sees us. Matt is too smart to sit for too long, waiting for her to be released, before he goes to the police."

"That's a lose end that could use tying up," Pagliano said. He started to hand the phone back to Braken, but withdrew it. "You got his number in here?" He scrolled through the contacts. "There you go ... Matty, how cute." He typed in a text to Matt. "He should be answering any second now. Let's get to the car and go find boy wonder."

* * *

Matt wandered aimlessly around the parking lot, not sure what to do. Sitting inside, watching the deputy fill out forms was not getting his mom back. Wanting his phone back, though, he walked around the building and knocked on the back door, hoping Justine would answer.

The intercom crackled. "Matt, that you?"

"Hey, let me in."

He stepped back as the door cracked open. "I'm not supposed to do this," she muttered.

"I need my phone."

"Just finished and gave it back to the deputy. Sorry, Matt. Can't get a line on your mom's phone. Must be dead or something."

Matt thought for a minute, and wondered if Will and Sheryl had missed him yet. It'd been at least ten minutes since he had walked outside. If he went in again, he suspected they might not let him leave again. "Justine, do me a solid and get the phone back. Tell him you thought of something else or something. I don't want to go back in there."

"Sure thing. Deputy dog gives me the creeps, anyhow. Hang out a minute. I'll be right back."

Matt waited by the door, thinking about his next move. He was so revved up he could feel the blood pulsing in his ears and felt useless hanging around here just waiting. Hopefully Justine would help.

The door opened a few minutes later and Justine poked her head out. She handed Matt the phone. "Here you go, Matt. Good luck."

He glanced at the screen hoping there was something about his mom. Just as he was about to look away a text came in from his grandfather. *Got your mom. Meet us at the Marina - all good.* His spirits lifted thinking his mom was safe. But he needed transportation. Will would give him a ride, but he didn't want to chance going back inside and being asked to stay for whatever reason deputy dog dreamed up. He looked at Justine "Cool. Hey, you got a bike here? I need to do something besides sit here and wait."

"Sure. It'll cost you later, though." She winked. "Wish I could have helped more. It's around the side there." She pointed to a concrete bollard protecting the electric meter. "Combo is 33533."

"Thanks." Matt turned to see if she was still there as he walked to the bike, he was met by her smile as the door shut. He fumbled with the lock, his trembling hands out of sync with his racing mind. Finally it came free and he stuck the U-shaped bracket on the seat stem. Before he took off, he texted his dad not knowing how, but hoping he could help. He knew that there was bad blood between them, but that his dad still cared for his mom. Maybe this would be some kind of wake up call for him.

Without looking back, he pedaled out to US 1, stopped at a

crosswalk, and checked his phone. The battery was at ten percent, but he didn't dare turn it off. Just as he was about to put it back in his pocket, it pinged with a message from his grandfather asking where he was. Hoping it was good news about his mom, he texted back that he was heading for the marina.

He tried to force Justine's smile from his mind and focus on what he had to do now as he peddled the two miles to the marina. The pink cruiser made the turn into the lot and coasted to a stop next to his grandfather's car. There were two people in the car; his grandfather behind the wheel, and a woman was in the passenger seat.

The window rolled down. "It's all right, Matt. We got her back," Braken said.

Her head turned towards him and Matt saw the bruises. "Mom! Are you okay?" He dropped the bike and ran around to the passenger side. Just as his hand touched the door handle, she ducked and a figure rose up from the backseat, a gun pointed at Matt's head.

The back door opened and Pagliano emerged, keeping the gun pointed at Matt. "In the car. Now."

Matt stood there in shock.

"Now, or she'll suffer more of the same." The gun motioned toward the backseat. Matt could see his mom through the window. She was injured and out of it. As he looked closer he could see her torn clothing and bruises. The only chance he had to help her was to do what the man said. If he ran off again he was sure Pagliano would inflict more damage. He moved toward the door and nodded his head for Matt to slide over. "Well, looks like we've got a family reunion. All except the drunk one, and he's probably lost in a bottle somewhere. Now, I'll take you up on that invitation to use your house, Braken."

* * *

Will and Sheryl alternated between sitting and pacing. He wanted to go outside and see what Matt was doing, realizing he'd been gone a while, but he was anxious something would happen the minute he stepped out. He glanced at the clock and calculated they had been there for almost an hour. Normally patient enough to sit out a tide change, he was tired of waiting. Matt needed his help. Figuring the boy would still be outside, he whispered something to Sheryl who nodded in understanding, stood and went to the door.

"Sheriff should be here anytime," the deputy called out from his desk.

His resolve faded, but with Sheryl behind him he couldn't turn back. "No problem, just getting some fresh air." He looked over at Sheryl. "Want to stretch your legs?"

She followed him outside, frowning. "Where'd Matt go? It's been a while."

"I don't know. He said he was just going to get some air. Matt!" he yelled. He waited for a response and then yelled again, starting to get concerned. "I'll go around this way. Why don't you take the other way and see if he's here?"

Will went to the right, Sheryl to the left. A short minute later they had checked the building.

"I didn't see him," she said as they met in front again.

"Me either," Will said. "What now?" He cursed himself for letting Matt get out of his sight. " He must have gotten impatient and went after Nicole by himself."

"But how? We drove him here."

"I don't know, but we need to find him. It's not good for him to be cruising around looking for her by himself. And what if he finds her? I don't think that scarface would think twice about hurting him. Or worse," he said.

"Let me tell the deputy we're going to grab a bite to eat, not that he'll care. At the rate they work, he'd still be filling out paperwork when we get back." She pulled on the handle.

"He's good," Sheryl said, as she emerged from the building. "But where would he have gone?"

"No idea. We can check his house or the marina, but I doubt he'll be at either place," Will said.

She stared at her phone, then gasped. "Will, I'm in a couple of groups around here, you know, kayaking and some environmental stuff. I just got some notifications that they are holding a protest out at Flamingo Key in the morning." She opened the link to the event and scrolled through the page. "There's a link to a video, but it doesn't work."

Will knew right away what it was, "That must have been the video Matt posted."

"Does it say anything else?"

"It's a big group to start with, but the RSVPs are already two pages long and still coming. Hey, you know I've seen Braken hanging around the group. There's a couple of guys like him - old guys trying to pick up young women. Guys like that give me the creeps - especially him."

"So, he would know too?"

"I think so. He would get the same messages I did."

Will thought for a minute. "That's going to force their hand. They'll have to do something and cover this up before then."

Sheryl looked back at her phone. "They are meeting at 8:00 tomorrow morning at the 54th Street ramp."

* * *

Braken walked up to his house with a gun at his back. Pagliano was behind the three hostages. "No lights." He held up his phone, moving it around the building. Like most homes in hurricane-prone areas, the house was built up on piers, with a carport and often a storeroom below. There was only one door for the enclosed space downstairs. Pagliano yanked on the knob, "Open it."

Braken withdrew a chain from his pocket and fumbled in the dark for the key. He saw Pagliano growing impatient, but that only increased his nervousness, and he dropped the ring.

"Pick it up and find the key." He pointed the gun at Matt.

Matt picked up the ring and started to try each in the lock. On the third try, the door swung open.

"In." He motioned with his gun. Braken went in first, followed by Matt, who was helping Nicole. Once they were inside, Pagliano closed the door and turned on the light. The room held the usual garage assortment of tools and hardware. He picked up a crowbar, turned off the light, and went outside, closing the door behind him. "You guys sit tight. I won't be long, gotta make a Home Depot run."

They heard a smash as the crowbar came down onto the lock.

Chapter 17

Joey Pagliano cruised the aisles of Home Depot, feeling out of place as he pushed the signature orange cart through the aisles. First stop was the outdoor garden area, where he loaded six bags of fertilizer with the highest nitrogen content he could find. Still outside, he located the pool chemicals, and added a case of muriatic acid to the cart. He'd spent several minutes on his phone in the parking lot, and pulled up a website that listed the top ten homemade bombs. The materials on his list were a combination of the most popular ingredients from his quick search. Later, he would spend some time on the proportions, but now he hustled through the store, loading up kerosene, acetone, some five-gallon buckets, and a couple of tiki torches. Surprised that he wasn't detained and Homeland Security called, he breezed through the checkout without the twenty-something inked up clerk giving him a second glance.

He loaded Braken's car with the materials and pulled out into traffic, trying to control his usual urge to speed. Either an accident or a ticket would be fatal to his plans. The former could blow the car, the latter land him in jail. The Meetup notification had accelerated his plans. Tomorrow morning he expected hundreds of people would be surrounding his island. And with these activists you never knew how long they were going to stay. Hell, he could see a commune being set up there. The evidence had to be destroyed before they showed up. Several minutes later, he pulled into Braken's driveway and parked under the carport. A quick check of the storeroom door showed no change.

"You guys in there?" he called out.

"Let us out of here!" Matt yelled.

Satisfied that they were under control, he went upstairs to finish his research, wincing when a security light came on as he was halfway up the stairs. Glancing toward it, he noticed a kayak hanging from two ropes. The image of Braken floating around in the plastic boat made him laugh out loud.

Maybe he could take out a bunch of the kayakers. There was going to be hell to pay with his bosses in Jersey, anyway. A little carnage was never a bad thing. Several years ago he had been exiled to Miami for a botched deal, and since then his results had not been stellar. The mob bosses didn't understand that there were different dynamics in South Florida. How could he generate the "no show" jobs they needed to show a W-2 to the IRS when there were no union jobs here to scam off. And everybody in real estate here was running some kind of scam. A lot of competition and half of them spoke another freakin' language. But a body count always seemed to satisfy them.

Once inside, he went to Braken's computer and turned it on. A porn site came on the screen as soon as it warmed up. He laughed as he minimized it and opened Google to finish his research. He looked like a college student taking notes as he scanned through site after site. Surprisingly, it took only three sites to piece together enough information to start assembly. The printer started its warmup and then spat out five pages, which he grabbed and took downstairs.

* * *

Will stood by the dock, wondering what their next move should be. He felt energized, but at the same time confused. Hero duty was not in his wheelhouse. Usually the guy on the side lines, he hadn't gotten in a fight since grade school. Now, with the police at a standstill, Matt missing, and Nicole in danger, he didn't know what to do. He looked at Sheryl, wondering if she sensed his inadequacies. *How could she not?* he thought. Quicksand could have been sucking him in for all the good he was doing.

"What'cha thinking?" she asked, moving toward him. "Looks like smoke's about to come out of your head."

"This is getting complicated, and I'm not sure what to do. I'm worried about the Meetup tomorrow. If something happens around that discharge pipe, it could get ugly. Makes sense now why I've seen so many sharks around there. We have no idea where Nicole or Matt are, and the sheriff hasn't even shown up yet."

She put a hand on his shoulder. "Any ideas?"

A picture of kayakers and chum floating around the island formed in his mind. "If that sewer discharge is putting out whatever you want to call it and all those boats are floating around it might bring in sharks. Why don't we cap it or something before the Meetup? It shouldn't be a big deal to do that. I've got some lights, we can grab some gear and go now. I hate to even say it, but if Scarface is really going to do something bad to Nicole and Matt, that's where he is going. He's out of time."

"I've been in the government long enough to know there are too many agencies that are going to want a piece of this. Even if the deputy gets off his butt and reports this, it'll be at least morning, maybe later, before they sort it out and get someone out there. It's a kidnapping now and the sheriff is going to wait for the FBI before they go out there. We may be the best chance to stop something bad from happening."

"Okay, the least we can do is fix the pipe," he said. "I've got supplies at my house. Why don't we take a ride there and get what we need." He drove the dark and quiet streets to his house deep in thought, feeling better that he might be able to actually do something. It was one thing to fix a pipe — he knew how to do that, but he did not have any idea how to handle a deranged mobster and wasn't sure he had the nerve to go through with it if he did. Whatever his reluctance, with Matt in jeopardy and the beautiful woman sitting next to him, with her hand on his knee, he knew the only way to go was forward. They drove in silence, both thinking about what lay ahead. He stopped in his driveway to open the gate. Once inside, he left the gate open and pulled up to the house. "It's kind of not done yet."

"Looks pretty awesome to me," she said as they got out of the car and he went to the stack of construction materials under the house.

He started to rummage through several piles as she walked away, apparently to check out the property. She seemed to instill confidence in him; even her small touches had settled him down. Or maybe it was not having to do this alone that reassured him. He tried to focus on the task at hand. From a pile of PVC fittings, he pulled out two caps, one for three-inch pipe, the other for four-inch.

"Love your place," she said, startling him.

He lost his train of thought. "Thanks. You can check out the house if you want, while I finish up here. There's probably some food in the refrigerator if you're hungry. Power's not on, but there's a flashlight by the door and some hurricane lamps around."

Crap, he thought. Something he had been thinking about when she interrupted had slipped his mind. Hoping it would come back to him, he finished assembling the materials and tools then went to the locked storeroom to get his dive gear. Mask, fins, BC, and regulator all came out of the room, along with a tank. Several wetsuits were hanging on the wall. The water was warm enough to skin dive, but he was hoping a covering of neoprene would give him some protection from the toxic discharge while he repaired the pipe, he selected the thinner three-millimeter suit. With the gear loaded into a laundry basket, he did a mental walk thru and realized he'd forgotten extra weight to compensate for the wetsuit.

Four pounds were in the pockets of his BC; what he needed for his body's buoyancy, and he searched around for another four pounds, needed to counteract the floatation of the wetsuit. Two weights and a dive light finally topped off the basket, which he set in the back of the truck, along with the tank and plumbing supplies.

Still thinking there was something he missed, he headed upstairs. The smell of bacon grilling on the camp stove greeted him as he opened the door.

"Hey. Hope you don't mind. I didn't realize how hungry I was."

His stomach groaned at the thought of food, and he realized he hadn't eaten since breakfast. "Sure, it's almost midnight. Breakfast sounds great."

He sat at the bar and watched her move through the kitchen. She seemed to know where everything was without asking. "I love this place. Even the camping thing. It's fun," she said as he took the offered plate. They quickly demolished the eggs, bacon, and cut fruit.

"We should probably get going. I'll get the dishes later."

"No. I will," she said with a smile.

* * *

Pagliano was back downstairs, having spread the supplies out in a line along the back of the house. He swatted the mosquitos that were swarming around him, attracted by the light he'd been forced to turn on. It was careless, but at this time of night and partially screened from the street, he hoped the light wouldn't attract attention.

It was time to build the bomb. First, he took the empty buckets and filled them two thirds of the way up with fertilizer. Next he dumped the acetone in, until the fertilizer was saturated. Anything else added at this point would be too combustible, so he put the lids on the buckets and loaded them in the trunk of the car with the rest of the supplies.

Using the flashlight to blind his captives, he opened the door to the storeroom. The crowbar prying the door open would have given them enough notice to plan an attack, though he doubted they would. But the light would stun them long enough to disrupt any plan they had. They instinctively covered their eyes when the light hit, and he smirked.

"Nothing funny, now. I've got you covered." He waved the gun with his other hand while still shining the light at them. "One at a time, out of here and into the car. Braken, in the passenger seat. Girl, you drive." He looked at her. "Anything happens, the boy gets it. I'll be in the back with him." They complied without question, just as he expected they would.

Nicole drove slowly, Pagliano making sure the speed limit was obeyed. They left Braken's neighborhood and turned onto US1. The only anxious moment came when they passed a police cruiser waiting for drunks, speeders, or both to come barreling down the road. They were neither, and Pagliano watched through the back window as the cruiser remained parked.

Chapter 18

Will drove quickly through the moonlit streets. A waning gibbous moon had just risen, lighting the cloudless sky.

"You sure you don't want to wait until daylight?" Sheryl asked.

"I think I'd rather get this done right now. Anyway, by the time we get out there the sun will be starting to rise, for now the moon will be directly overhead. We should be good."

"Sorry. I just worry about stuff sometimes."

"You? I'm the worry guy." He tried to give her a reassuring smile, and extended his hand toward hers. Their fingers locked. He thought for a minute. "You go on some of those Meetups?"

"Yeah, usually they're fun. Some people are pretty cool, but some are creepers. You know, like that Braken guy. Tried to hit on me a couple of times. Then he walks in the building department the other day and doesn't even recognize me."

"Maybe we can do that sometime," he said.

"I think I'd rather have you to myself," she slid closer.

The marina was deserted when they pulled in a few minutes later. Will pulled up to the dock, got out, and started to unload the truck. Once everything was out, he asked Sheryl to start taking stuff to the boat and he got back in the truck. She gave him a questioning look but did as he asked. Several minutes later, he came jogging back to the dock.

"Just wanted to stash the car. If Braken and Scarface are going out there, I don't want them to see my truck."

"Won't they see that the boat's missing?"

"Maybe, maybe not. Not sure they'll be looking for my boat in particular." Will grabbed a load of the remaining gear and headed for the dock. Once the boat was loaded he lashed down the tank and stashed the gear and supplies.

The engine started, breaking the predawn silence, and he winced as several birds flew screeching from the trees. Will waited while Sheryl tossed the dock lines onto the dock. Once clear, he backed the boat out of the slip. The bow sliced through the water, gently disrupting the even pattern of the wind ripples on the surface.

Out of habit he had the radio on. Tuned to channel two, the NOAA weather report for the Florida Keys came through the speaker. Weather was just one more thing to add onto the list of decomposing bodies, sharks, and mobsters. A fast moving front was forecast to hit the area. The calm conditions they experienced now wouldn't last. He was getting anxious as they idled through the canal and reached open water, the moon lighting the water and giving him enough security to put the boat on plane. The light hull jumped as he pushed on the throttle, quickly leveling out and skimming over the small waves.

They watched the lights of the shore pass in silence, and Will slowed when they neared the Key. He turned on the depth finder and idled toward the shore, trying to remember the spot where the pipe extended out from the island.

A novice might have missed the small hump on the display, but Will saw it and turned parallel with the pipe. Continuing to idle, he drove about four hundred yards, to where he suspected the pipe was broken. The depth finder showed twelve feet of water under the boat. "You know how to drive this?"

"I've driven a jet ski," she said.

Not sure whether it was better to anchor and move the boat once he'd found the break, or let her follow him, he decided on anchoring. She didn't sound very sure of herself, and in skinny water the spinning propeller would be a real potential for injury if the boat weren't in experienced hands. He went forward, opened a hatch, and removed the anchor, its chain hitting the deck as he pulled the line out. It slid off the deck and splashed into the water.

"I'm going to gear up. You going to be okay up here by yourself?"

She nodded. "How long do you think you'll be down there?"

"Might be a while. I have to follow the pipe until I find the break, mark the spot, and come back."

"I'm a little nervous, but…"

They came together in a quick embrace, her hold tighter than he expected. He reluctantly broke it off and pulled on the wetsuit. With the tank behind him on the deck, he slipped on the BC, fished around behind his back with his right arm to retrieve the regulator, set it in his mouth, and checked the airflow. Rising, he sat on the gunwale and checked the air gauge. A thumbs up sign and loud splash indicated his entry into the water.

It was dark and murky. Will turned on the light and descended to the sandy bottom, moving the dive light back and forth over the bottom illuminating the turtle grass swaying with the current. He realized how fortunate he was that it was a slack tide; if he'd attempted this when the water was moving, the visibility, now only a few feet, would have been zero.

The light found the barnacle-crusted pipe and he began to swim along side it. A couple of hundred yards later he found the break. A T-fitting had been installed, probably as a clean out. A small section of pipe extended from the top. Where it should have had a cap, the pipe was open. He shivered as small particles floated from the opening. Until now he had been focused only on the pipe, but in a moment of panic he spun 360 degrees, light extending out into the water beyond him. He hadn't thought about the fact that he was going to be swimming right in the chum slick. He could only pray that there weren't any predators out there right now.

Gulping, he reached into the pocket of his BC and removed what looked like a small dumbbell. It was a small length of PVC pipe, capped at both ends with foam cut from a swim noodle taped around it for flotation. Wound around the center was a weighted line, which he unclipped from the pipe.

He had just released the line and dropped the weight on the buoy when something brushed his leg. Startled he gave a quick squirt of air into the BC and rose to the surface. It would have been faster to submerge and follow the pipe back, but the thought of whatever had just bumped him, and Sheryl alone in the boat, was enough to send him up. He turned on his back and finned hard toward the boat, where she helped him by grabbing the top of the tank as he pulled himself over the transom.

Back on board, he slipped out of his gear, and moved to the helm. Idling slowly toward the anchor he created enough slack in the line that she could pull it. Once retrieved, they moved toward the buoy and reset the anchor.

* * *

Braken stood behind Pagliano, holding a flashlight on the bundle of wires pulled from the clips that held them in place on the engine. He watched as the gangster followed the wires one at a time, trying to find the two that would start the engine when touched together.

"How are we going to start this thing? Back in the day, I could hot wire anything, but if I cut the wrong wire, this boat ain't moving." Pagliano put the cowling back on the engine.

"Let me go look in the cabin, maybe he has a key stashed in there." Braken went for the small door in the center of the console and tried to push it open, but it wouldn't budge. "It's locked."

"Where's your boy?" Pagliano asked Braken.

"Hell, it's the middle of the night. He's probably home in bed."

"Go. Get him — now. I'll stay here and keep your family company while you're gone. I don't need to remind you what'll happen if there's any funny business. Do I?"

Braken shook his head. Besides what Pagliano was sure to do to Nicole and Matt, he knew that a jail cell awaited him for his role as an accomplice.

He walked toward the car, and slumped against the wheel, the stress and lack of sleep and food were taking a toll on him. He could only hope Cody would be home.

The car backed out of the space, and turned onto the road. Several minutes later, his heart fell into his stomach as he pulled up to Cody's house. The driveway was empty. *He could still be here*, he thought. *Maybe someone drove him home*. Doubting it, he got out and banged on the door and waited impatiently for an answer. After several attempts, he tried the handle. Locked. He followed the wrap-around deck to the back door and tried the knob to the side door.

The door opened into the dark house. Lights illuminated his path as he flicked switches and moved through the house, going toward the master bedroom. His stomach dropped further when he turned on the light and found the bed empty. Cody was not here and he had no other plan. He sat on the bed, head in hands thinking about Matt and Nicole alone with Pagliano. If Cody showed up while he was gone they might leave without him and there was no telling what could happen then. He tried Cody's number again, but it went straight to voicemail. He left the lights on as he left the house and went for his car.

The house receded in his rear view mirror as he drove away, still not knowing what to do. Then he remembered something. It was a shot in the dark, but it might work. During the boom of the early 2000s, he had owned a used boat lot. Outboard engines had only a handful of keys for each model, not an individual key like cars used. Maybe he had a key that fit Cody's boat.

He drove quickly to his house, hoping it would work. Once inside, he grabbed a bottle of water, an energy bar, and a ring full of keys. He ran out the door and was back on the road, eating the bar when the police car lights flashed behind him. Enraged by his stupidity he started to pull over. The cruiser had been there before, but he had forgotten and now cursed himself for forgetting. Just as he was envisioning himself in jail, the car sped past. Once the Highway patrol car had gone, he sped up again and drove to the marina. There were two other cars there now — the beginning of the day's activity — and the sun was starting to brighten the sky from just below the horizon.

He ran to the dock, hoping he hadn't been gone long enough to incur Pagliano's wrath. Behind the helm, he frantically tried each key, losing hope as the first several did nothing. Matt, Nicole, and Pagliano looked on as he went through the key chain.

Finally one turned, and the motor started.

Chapter 19

Cody, startled by the motor starting, jumped up and smacked his head against the decomposing headliner in the cabin. Insulation rained around him as he tried to figure out where he was and what was going on. He moved to the cabin window and peeled back the curtain. Dawn was breaking, the sun's reflection just visible on the water and the dock was receding as the boat headed out toward the gulf. Nausea overcame him, forcing him to lay back down.

His head pounded from the long night of drinking. The boat was his home on those nights; it was a short walk from the bar, and in his usual state of consciousness, pretty comfortable. Days he had a charter he could slip around the back of the storeroom adjacent to the office and use the outside shower there. It was cold water, but had the desired effect, removing the cobwebs from the night before.

As he lay on the bunk, he tried to make out the voices coming from the cockpit. It sounded like two men talking, but he couldn't be sure. What the hell was going on out there, and who was stealing his boat? He sat up slowly, waited a minute for his head and stomach to catch up and then rose to a stoop. The cabin ceiling was shorter than his six-foot height, so he crouched, ear to the door, and listened.

One voice came through clearer than the other, or maybe it was because he knew it better. It was his father. The other remained a mystery. Just as he was about to open the cabin door, another wave of nausea hit him, forcing him back to the bunk.

* * *

Doug stood on the boat ramp next to his kayak. He liked to be first to these outings, ready to greet everyone and make new connections. A large coffee in his hand, he was ready for the day. The line of cars, most carrying kayaks, wove its way into the parking area. He smiled as he looked at the line of vehicles, already out of the parking area and starting to encroach onto the road.

A large turnout was essential to accomplish his goals. He had sent press releases late last night to all the media from Key West to Miami, but he didn't expect anything to come from them by themselves. Unless there was a curious reporter with time on their hands, it was just planting a seed. A large enough crowd would ensure *some* kind of police communication, and the media all monitored law enforcement channels. They would put two and two together. Best case was a helicopter flyover and some footage for the evening news. That kind of video would find its way instantly to the Internet, flooding YouTube and Facebook with posts and links.

It would draw all the attention he wanted. Guerrilla activism in the digital age.

Several regular members came up and greeted him. They had the routine down. Get there early, unload quickly, and park. The limited number of parking spaces at the boat ramp were already gone. Doug had a plan, and reserved several spaces with the traffic cones he kept in the back of his Subaru Outback for volunteers willing to run a shuttle for the late comers to have a coveted parking space.

The sun was over the horizon now, about seven o'clock, and already things were better than he had expected. Satisfied this was going to be the success he had hoped for, he got to work helping newcomers unload their boats and get situated. When he looked up after an hour, he was shocked to see the entire lot covered in a multi-colored canvas of kayaks.

At 7:45 he went for the closest picnic table to the ramp, climbed on top, and yelled for quiet. It took a few minutes to settle the large crowd, and while he waited for silence, he tried to guess how many people were there. Crowds were easiest to estimate if you broke out a group of ten or so people, took the area they encompassed, and applied that formula to the rest of the crowd. It wasn't dead accurate, but he was shocked when he counted twenty groups. A flotilla with two hundred boats could ring the entire Key. That would be the spectacle he sought.

"Attention everyone!" he yelled, sensing the moment he would be heard. "Thank y'all for coming. Now with this many people, we need to keep things organized. Let's all break into groups of ten and stay together. Our goal is Flamingo Key. I'm guessing most of you saw the YouTube video. There's a group here that is trying to sell off parcels of land to build homes on that beautiful island. They are trying to market them as sustainable. But we know," he paused to get their attention, "that any building in this fragile environment is unsustainable. Birds live there, dolphins play there — it is theirs more than ours. Now, let's go out there and show these people that we care, and they will have to fight us to ruin these pristine lands."

He grabbed a handful of laminated papers from a box besides him, "I have enough charts for every group to take one." Eager boaters started to line up and take them from his outstretched hands. "When we get out there, we are going to spread out and circle the island. Anyone with a phone or camera, get a shot or a video. When we get back we'll flood the Internet and everyone will know about this. Be safe people!"

They started out in their groups, paddles bobbing back and forth in the water. He went with the last group, staying behind to ensure that any late comers would know their plan. Satisfied he was the last boat out, he started to paddle quickly, using his core to move his arms. Most of the paddlers were not as experienced, and used what he called girlie arms to paddle. His technique propelled him forward: keep your arms straight, push with the lead hand, and a good twist were the keys to power.

He quickly reached the front group and took the lead. The waterproof VHF radio clipped under a bungee on the deck let out a call every few minutes. Several power boats were forced to change course by the long string of boats, while others stopped and gawked at the spectacle. Finally a sheriff's boat appeared on the horizon and started idling by the line of kayakers. Doug smiled when he heard the request for several Coast Guard Auxiliary boats to come out and monitor the convoy.

With this much chatter and attention, he was going to get his news helicopter.

* * *

Will strapped the tank to his back after assembling the parts in a mesh bag set at his feet. The PVC fittings clanked in the bag as he moved toward the gunwale, and handed it to Sheryl, not wanting to lose it on entry.

"Can you toss me this when I'm in?" He looked at the bag, then, and remembered what he had forgotten at the house: The waterproof PVC cement. "What was I thinking?" he gasped. "This will never work underwater." He pulled the can out and handed it to her.

"Why don't you dry fit everything you can, and bring the pieces up for me to glue? That should leave just one connection unglued. I'll see what I can come up with for that."

He gave her a questioning glance, and she grinned.

"My father was a plumber."

He put the regulator in his mouth and started to breath while he gathered the hoses against his body. One hand on the regulator the other on his chest to hold the equipment in place he fell backwards into the water. The visibility had increased dramatically, now that the sun had risen. It was close to ten feet now — pretty good for this shallow on the bay side. He had chosen to dive without fins this time, as there was no need to swim, and even the smallest movement would silt up the water, decreasing the visibility.

The extra weight he had added took him to the bottom where he found the pipe. Kneeling in the sand with the mesh bag beside him, he went to work. With a small handsaw he started to cut the pipe. It was harder work than he anticipated with the water providing resistance. Bubbles rose in a thick stream as he worked, a sign he was using air rapidly. It shouldn't be an issue in only twelve feet of water and he dismissed the thought.

Will did as Sheryl asked and assembled a coupling to a small, cut piece of pipe, then added a cap at the end. He tested it on the freshly cut pipe and surfaced. She grabbed the assembly from him as he reached over the transom, then held onto the boat as she glued the pieces together.

The procedure was taking longer than he'd hoped, and he scanned the horizon for boats. Toward land, he saw what looked like a flock of birds on the surface of the water. Studying the unusual sight, he noticed what he was seeing was not birds, but paddles, which were reflecting the water dripping from them in the sunlight.

"Hey, look over there. You're higher up, hop on the poling platform and see what it is."

She turned from her work and looked where he was pointing. The platform elevated her four feet above the water, plus her five-foot-eight height, and she was able to see much more than he could in the water.

She took a long look, then came back down, her expression worried. "It's the kayak Meetup thing. There must be a couple hundred of them."

Will didn't want to be in the area when they got there. He didn't want them prowling around the pipe or mistaking him for one of the developers. They didn't need to know what was going on. He had wanted to fix the pipe and be gone before anyone arrived to ask questions. "We have to finish fast."

She handed the glued up pipes to him. He submerged again and went back to work, eyeing the gathering school of barracuda attracted by the activity and free breakfast from the pipe. Although barracuda didn't worry him, he thought about the larger predators the chum slick might bring in. With all this activity going on, he was sure that unless he could cap the pipe, that sharks were bound to appear. Hoping it would hold, he jammed the pipe into the fitting, frustrated at the amount of time this was taking, and finally surfaced again.

"It's capped for now."

Sheryl didn't answer, but he heard her talking. He swam around the boat to see what was going on, quickly submerging before his head hit the two kayaks hovering by the boat.

Chapter 20

"Holy crap. Look at those idiots." Pagliano yelled.

They were about a quarter mile from Flamingo Key. Braken was at the helm of the Grady-White racing across the flat water at twenty-five knots. He looked toward the right, over the starboard gunwale at the cluster of kayaks ringing the Key. They were still a quarter mile away when Pagliano signaled for him to slow. The boat rocked back as the propeller stopped.

"What the fuck do those passion-fruit-tea-drinking sons of bitches think they're doing? We've gotta break this up before one of them decides to check out the flora or whatever the fuck they do."

Nicole and Matt sat huddled on the deck, Matt holding her tightly. "They have as much right to be there as you do," Matt said.

Pagliano went toward the stern and kicked him. "I want a comment from you, I'll be sure to put it on YouTube. You realize this is all your fault?"

Braken broke the tension, desperate to pacify Pagliano. Watching his family being abused was changing his opinion of his associate. There would be more deals with better partners — if he could survive this one. He wondered where Cody was, hoping that he had at least discovered that the boat was missing, and maybe gotten off his hungover ass and done something about it. "So, what do you want to do?"

"We've gotta break it up. You know, make 'em scatter."

Braken thought for a minute. It would be easy to spook the

kayakers — just a couple of high-speed flybys would swamp a few in his wake. That would probably be enough to scare them without hurting anyone. But there was the problem of him being seen at the wheel of the boat. Many people, both from this group and the area, knew him by sight. Many of them had been burned in his deals, and wouldn't need an excuse to turn him in. His only hope was people would assume it was Cody at the helm. *Hope the boy has an alibi,* he thought.

"I can run in and swamp a couple, that'll break up the party."

"Now you're talking," Pagliano said. "Could even be some fun."

Braken turned the boat toward the Key and pushed down on the throttle. It jumped up on plane and flew toward the group while he hunched over, trying to hide himself as he closed in on them. The boat slowed slightly as Braken turned to angle the boat's wake for a direct hit. The first wave reached the group and lifted the small boats onto its crest before plummeting them into the two-foot trough. Several of the more experienced kayakers used their paddles to brace into the wave, stabilizing the craft. Most, with less training, tried to use their body weight to level off the craft. It was the second group that capsized. Paddles flashed in the sun as the other boaters raced to help the victims.

"That was excellent. Do it again!" Pagliano yelled over the engine noise.

Braken turned the boat and broadsided another group with an even larger wave. He grinned as five or six more boats dumped their occupants into the water. Damned environmental assholes deserved this. Focused on the chaos, he forgot about Nicole and Matt, and made another run at the kayakers. Many were panicking, sitting in place waiting for someone to help, others were turning toward shore and paddling hard. He started after a pod of boats, sitting still, bickering with each other, but Pagliano stopped him.

"Hear that?" He yelled.

"What?" Braken strained to hear, eventually pulling the throttle back until it clicked in neutral. He heard it then: A helicopter flying fast and low, approaching from the east. He glanced up, squinting to try to find it. "Looks like a Miami TV chopper," he said.

"We've done enough. Let's blast on oughta here before they get close enough and start shooting footage of us. I don't think we want to make the news."

Braken pushed the throttle hard and turned the wheel, making a huge wave, which swamped a few more boats. Before the chopper could reach the Key, they were a mile away.

"Stick some rods out. Make it look like we're just a bunch of folks out here fishing in case they fly over." He reached for the two rods stashed under the side of the boat. Pagliano gave him a questioning look. "Never fished huh? Sure made a lot of chum though," Braken laughed, high on adrenaline, forgetting for the moment the danger he and his family were in.

The mobster quickly caught on and grabbed the rods. He fumbled with the bales trying to let line out, finally he succeeded and they sat under the shade of the Bimini top which kept them hidden from the helicopter. Both rods were cast out and set in rod holders when the chopper flew over, the blades pounding the air downward, disturbing the water. With nothing to be seen here, it quickly moved on and hovered over Flamingo Key.

* * *

Will and Sheryl had been caught in the middle of the chaos. They were doing their best to help the more inexperienced kayakers back into their boats. Will reached over the low freeboard of the flats boat and righted the upside-down boats while Sheryl used the pole to bring the swimmers back to their craft. He knew it was Cody from the shape of the Grady-White and wondered why he had ignored their boat in his frenzy leaving them in the middle

123

of the fracas. Other, more experienced boaters were performing their own rescues. It looked like a giant self rescue clinic. He had tried to see who else was aboard the Grady-White, but the screams and turmoil surrounding them distracted him. By the time he had a chance to look again the boat was gone, remnants of its wake showing its course.

"That was the boat from the other night wasn't it?" Sheryl asked as they moved toward another stranded boater.

"Yeah, that's Cody's boat. This is going to kill their investment scam when word gets out." He pointed to the helicopter. "That's not in their best interest, either." He kept the more gruesome thought to himself: that Matt and Nicole might have been aboard the boat. As things escalated there was no telling how Braken and scarface would react.

"I wonder where the sheriff is. I can't believe they're not out here." She put the pole back in its holder.

"I don't know. I say we head back in and go find them and report this. We were eyewitnesses, and it was definitely Cody's boat. If I were him, I'd be on my way to a hidey hole out in the backcountry and come in after dark. I don't think he'll be heading in soon. That pipe's capped for now, and just in time. With that chum line running and all the kayakers flailing in the water, sharks would have zeroed in fast." Finally he felt like he had actually accomplished something.

"I guess that was good timing, at least." She went to him and squeezed his arm, and they looked toward the Key. Only a handful of kayaks remained; the rest were paddling back toward shore. They'd had enough, and their protest was effectively over before it started. He checked the boat, making sure the tank and dive gear were secure before pushing the throttle down.

* * *

Cody was starting to get hungry. His hangover had faded

into the past as he watched his father swamp all those kayaks. He had laughed out loud at the spectacle, moving from one side of the cabin to the other to check out all the action. Now, he wondered what was going on. He could tell they were anchored by the way the boat swung in the current, but no landmarks were visible from the windows. Searching through the drawers, he found some peanuts and drank some water from the hose by the head. It was quiet now, without the motor running, and he could hear voices on the deck. The same two men as before — one his father for sure. But now there were two others, and he was sure they were Nicole and Matt. What were they doing aboard with Joey Pagliano? he wondered. Their voices were muted, but he sensed the stress.

He looked around for someway to find out what was happening and settled on the fresh air vent mounted in the ceiling. Slowly, he cranked the handle. Wishing he had done some maintenance on the unit, he cringed as it groaned with every turn, but it was forward of the cabin so unless someone were looking directly at it, it wouldn't be noticed. One turn at a time he cranked it and the square plastic lid raised an inch with each turn. The voices were clearer now, and he thought he heard Nicole crying and Matt trying to comfort her. Braken and Pagliano were fighting about whether to go back to the Key or the marina. Braken wanted to wait until nightfall — *probably the right choice*, Cody thought, given what they'd just done. Pagliano wanted to go back to the island and finish what they came for, whatever that was.

Matt said something that he couldn't make out, and then he heard Nicole scream. Without a second thought, he threw the slide bolt that locked the door from the inside and barged through the opening, catching Pagliano in the back. He landed on top of him and started to slam his fists into the mobster's head. Nicole came over and slammed the prone man with a billy club, used to knock out fish, on the back of his head, leaving him motionless on the deck. They looked at each other holding the gaze for a moment until the body moved.

"Quick!" Cody yelled to Matt. "Get me something to tie him

with! A dock line or leader, quick!" He needed to move fast —
Pagliano was coming to.

Matt rummaged through the cluttered compartments, trying
to find anything that might work, and finally handed two nylon
cable ties to Cody.

One tie went around the wrists, the other around Pagliano's
feet. Once he was secured, Cody stood, went to Matt and hugged
him. "Thought I was going to lose you." He turned next to Nicole.
"And you too," he said, embracing her, surprised that she didn't
pull back

Chapter 21

Will saw the remnants of the Grady-White's wake ahead of them. In seconds the wake would disperse and there would be no way of knowing where they had gone. Heading towards Big Pine, he knew there were enough small keys they could lose themselves. Smugglers had been hiding out for centuries here. They could land at any one of those islands, camouflage the boat, and disappear until their supplies ran out. He evaluated his options. Looking back he saw the danger to the kayakers had passed and most were paddling back to shore. The probability of Matt being aboard the Grady tipped the scales towards action. "We need to go after them. I'm pretty sure Matt is with them and the water's too skinny for the sheriff to get their boat in there."

"What are we going to do when we find them?" She looked panicked.

He tried to reassure her, "Just keep an eye on them — from a distance. Can you call the sheriff and tell them the kayakers are safe and that we are going to follow the Grady-White and get back to them with a location."

"Sure," she reached for her phone and dialed. Turning away, she shielded the phone from the building wind and Will couldn't hear the conversation. She disconnected and turned back to him. "They were on the other side of the Key helping kayakers. They're wanting to know what bearing they're heading — they'll follow."

Will was relieved the sheriff was on scene now. He looked at the compass and called out to Sheryl, "Two hundred fifty degrees. I'd bet he's heading for the mangroves off East Bahia Honda or just past to Hardup Key. That's where I'd go."

"Run from the law much," she prodded, then called the bearing in.

He ignored the remark as she sidled closer. There was not a fishermen who had ever been out here that hadn't dreamed of being a pirate holed up in the backcountry. As they followed the diffusing wake, Will looked over his shoulder.

"What do you keep looking at?"

"Winds building and look back there. You can see the line of the cold front coming. Things are going to get nasty when that moves through." He strained to see the wake now as the seas built. It looked like the Grady-White had changed course to the northwest to stay clear of the Red Bay Bank. Will thought for a second. Then he would cut through to the safety of the Elbow Banks and East Bahia Honda, he guessed.

"Where are you going? It looks like they went that way," she pointed at the horizon.

"The chop is going to make it impossible to see their wake in a few minutes. I think I know where they're going and with this boat," he patted the wheel, "I can skirt some of the shallower water and come in from the north where he won't be looking.

* * *

The sun blinded Pagliano as he tried to open his eyes. He quickly shut them and rolled his head to the side. Wrists and feet bound, he struggled to a sitting position. Getting out of the restraints would not be a problem. Cable ties, he knew, came in two grades. The hardware store variety — which he was sure these were — could be cut by friction. Law enforcement ties were another story. He looked around for anything that might help and saw the braided fishing line spooled onto a reel near his head. That would work, he'd just have to be patient and wait for an opportunity. Confident he could get out of his restraints when they were not looking, he focused on how to complete his plan. All he had to do was break free, run back to the island, and toss them in the tank before he blew it. Then take the boat up to Key Largo and call Miami for a pickup. Piece of cake.

But the odds at four of them against him, even with his experience, were not optimal. Better to set them against each other.

He observed their interactions. Truly a dysfunctional family, he watched the older man coddle Nicole and Matt. *That wouldn't last long*, he thought. Braken and Cody were too narcissistic to pay anyone else attention for too long. His best bet was to let things go until they got bored with giving attention to someone else, and then go to work. His opening came sooner than he expected. Braken was already sitting to the side, looking at his phone.

"You know this is going to go bad for you," he said. "Miami finds out about you guys tying me up and you'll be in the tank for sure."

Braken tried to ignore him, but Pagliano knew he had his attention.

"You're the one going in the tank," Cody yelled at him. He was still hovering over Nicole. "How could you do this?"

"Do what? Bitch got in the way. Wait till I get to you."

Pagliano caught Matt looking to the north and followed his gaze toward the sound of an engine approaching. He could see the spray the bow put up as it cut through the waves, but the hull remained invisible.

"I think we ought to call the sheriff and turn him over," Matt said.

"Bad idea, son. Your dad and I are too deep in this. They'd never understand," Braken said.

Pagliano saw his opening, "You know, Braken, I could forget the last hour or so if you untie me and we finish off the tank. I'll give your family a pass too."

"No way, Grandpa, don't trust him," Matt sneered.

"Boy's right," Cody said. "Only way I see getting out of this is to do to him what he wanted to do to us. Then blow that thing and call it good."

Pagliano was surprised by Cody's reasoning. Maybe the boy had some potential after all. He watched the group as their heads nodded in ascent. *Not so bad, really,* he thought. *It'll be way easier to take them if I can get off this boat.* His immediate concern was the restraints. Somehow he needed to get out of sight for a few minutes and fashion a cutting device. The braided fishing line he had seen would work well. Slowly he shimmied his body and made his way toward the cabin.

"Where are you going?" Cody asked.

"Just trying to get out of the sun," Pagliano replied. Another few feet and most of his body would be blocked by the cabin.

"Let him be," Braken said. "He's tied up."

Pagliano stayed put until Cody relaxed and went back toward Nicole. He needed to remain as unthreatening as possible. Matt and Nicole went below, and soon appeared to be asleep on one of the bunks. Braken slouched in the chair at the helm, also asleep. Cody was fidgety. He started fishing, then went back and forth to check on Matt and Nicole, then back to check the lines.

Pagliano started to nod off himself, the afternoon heat and lack of water making him sleepy. As long as Cody was wearing a path over the deck, he had no chance to escape. *Might as well save energy,* he thought. Getting as comfortable as possible, he started to doze.

* * *

The deputy behind the wheel steered clear of the sandbar, careful to give the twenty-seven-foot Contender the draft it required. The specs called it nineteen inches of clearance, but that was empty and without the added depth of the engine and propellors. Three feet was the skinniest water he was going to take the boat in, and that forced him well clear of the flat where they suspected the Grady-White was anchored.

"Can't you get any closer?" the sheriff asked.

He looked over at her. Jules was a fixture in Marathon, and had been sheriff since returning from Iraq in the mid 90's. Well respected, she had one fatal flaw in his eyes: She was a golfer, not a boater. "Need to stay in three-plus feet of water. Tide's out now too. Maybe at high tide we could get close." He looked at his watch. "But that's not until midnight. Sun will be setting soon. He'll probably make his move then."

"Let's just maintain recon for now. The woman called someone on her phone. "They had them in sight on the other side of the mangroves. They'll call us if they move. Stay out of sight, and watch him through the binoculars."

The deputy released the windlass, waited until the anchor line slacked, and started backing up. Once enough scope was out, he locked the line and stopped the boat. The anchor grabbed the sandy bottom.

He surveyed the flat with his binoculars. "Can't see much with these. They're too far away. Looks like maybe three of them, but I can't make out any faces."

Jules set the rifle to her shoulder and looked through the scope. "Got three. Braken's at the wheel. Looks like his son is there, and I can just make out another body on the deck. No sign of his daughter or the boy."

"Too bad you can't just pick them off, one at a time and end this," he said.

"Yeah, a few less Brakens around, you might not have a job," she joked.

Chapter 22

Cody waited until the lower edge of the sun hit the horizon to pull the anchor. Nicole and Matt were still asleep in the cabin. He had woken Braken, given him direction how to steer, and was at the bow, ready to grab the anchor line as soon as the boat moved forward enough to allow enough slack to retrieve it. Pagliano's head rose from the deck as soon as the motor fired.

"Forward a hair. Not too much or we'll ground," Cody called out from the bow, carefully watching the water below the boat. The tide was close to its lowest point and while that had kept the sheriff away, it was going to make things more difficult to get out. There was only one small channel that would accommodate the draft of his boat now.

The anchor came in easily, and he called to Braken to reverse and then idle. Once the anchor was secure, he went to the helm and took over. It took several maneuvers to turn the one hundred eighty degrees needed to hit the narrow channel and escape the flat. With only one outboard he had to perform a tight three-point turn, like a car in a narrow street. He started to search for the darker areas, marking the deeper cut. The boat idled forward and he exhaled now that they were ensconced in deep blue water. He pushed down on the throttle and opened up the 225 HP engine. Nicole and Matt came up from the cabin, rubbing sleep from their eyes. He glanced over at them and saw that both looked better for the rest.

"Where are we going, Cody? The marina is over there." Her voice was raspy as she pointed at the horizon. These were the first words she had spoken since he had burst out of the cabin and subdued Pagliano.

"Going to Flamingo Key, babe," he said. "Gonna finish this mess off for good. Our boy here," he said, looking at Pagliano tied up and huddled on the deck, "He has a bunch of homemade explosives. Best thing for this family is to make the whole damned thing go away — him included."

"Are you sure that's such a good idea? We can just go in and turn him into the sheriff," she said.

"No, we're doing this my way. Too much risk that he makes a phone call from jail and sends his buddies after us."

She looked wary, but was swayed by his reasoning. "That's fine. He's a freakin' beast anyway." Her head swung to the right, "Who's boat is that?"

Cody followed her gaze and surveyed the horizon. The Key was less than a quarter mile away, and he could see a small flats boat idling toward the eastern point. "Son of a bitch," he smacked the wheel. "Can't catch a break. That's Will." He slowed the boat and spun the wheel toward the other side of the island. "We can try and wait him out. He's probably scared of the dark."

* * *

Will watched them pull anchor and headed towards them. He immediately pulled the pole that he had used to anchor his boat in the shallow water from the sandy bottom and set it on the deck. "We gotta move quick. They're coming right at us." The boat turned and was on plane and running at close to thirty knots in seconds. He continued north towards deeper water. "Can you call the sheriff," he ducked to avoid the spray from a wave they had just plowed through. "Tell them I think they're heading back to Flamingo Key," He had to yell to be heard. On top of the engine noise the wind and seas had both picked up.

"But we're going the wrong way."

"He's got to come out this way now. It's the bottom of the tide," he said, ducking again and taking her with him to avoid the sheet of water coming over the bow. Despite their best efforts they were both wet now from the spray kicked up by the hull as it plowed into the white-capped waves. Will turned back towards land following at a distance as the Grady-White emerged from the mangroves and turned. They were far enough back that only the boat's antennas were visible above the building waves. Will was confident that the lower profile of his boat kept them safe from detection. Once the island came into view, he closed enough to see the Grady-White turn towards the beach.

"Can you see anything?" he asked Sheryl as he leaned around the windscreen now obscured with salt.

She climbed onto the poling platform and knelt, keeping one hand on its edge for balance, "Not sure. The boat's anchored off the mangroves and it looks like someone's unloading something."

"Let's take a peek. I can go around the other end. We'll be coming upwind so they won't hear the engine."

The shoreline came into view an inch at a time as he slowly moved around the point. He backed off just as the Grady-White came into view, turned the wheel toward shore, and moved forward again. From this angle, they could see the boat, but were hidden by the mangroves. They both moved toward the starboard side of the boat and watched.

Relief washed over him when he saw Matt and Nicole were still alive. Braken and Matt were on the beach, a cluster of five-gallon buckets at their feet. Cody was unloading another from the boat.

"What do you think?" she asked.

"They all look okay. One happy family," Will replied. They watched as the last bucket joined the others on the beach, and Braken went back with Cody to the boat and talked to Nicole. She climbed over the transom and into the water. Together, they waded to the beach and joined Matt. The men picked up a bucket in each hand, while Matt and Nicole grabbed the tiki torches and jugs. They moved single file toward the center of the island.

"We've got to stop them," Will said. "There's no telling what's in those buckets, but it can't be good. With that pipe still not sealed, they could kill off everything within miles of here."

* * *

"There he goes." Jules ran toward the bow and started to pull on the anchor line.

"Easy, chief, stand back." The deputy hit the switch, activating the windlass, and the anchor pulled easily from the soft bottom, the line coiling around the automatic windlass and dropping into the compartment.

She gave him a *whatever* look and moved next to the leaning post. Seconds later, she grabbed the stainless steel piping of the superstructure as the boat took off. "Don't get up on him too fast," she yelled into the deputy's ear. "The woman said they were heading back to Flamingo Key. We have to be patient and not spook him. I'm calling in some backup."

The boat slowed as the island came into view. "Looks like he went around the backside," the deputy yelled.

"There's another boat over there. Must be that woman and her boyfriend." She pointed toward the point. "Not sure what he's up to, but it looks like they are watching him. Let's sit here for a few and see how this unfolds." She got on her radio and called for the two other sheriff's boats to move into position; one a half mile behind them, the other circling to take up station on the other side of the Key. That way they would have eyes everywhere. She tried to call the woman on her cell phone, but there was no answer.

Catching them on land was more appealing to her than trying to stop the boat and board them at sea. She had thought about putting the helicopter up, it might spook their prey. She wanted to catch them in the act of whatever they had planned.

Chapter 23

Pagliano rolled to his knees as soon as they were out of sight, the movement rehearsed in his head for the last hour. The spinning reel loaded with braided line was within a few inches of his hands. Slowly, he moved toward it and peeled off several feet of line. It was slow work, with both his hands and feet bound, but when he was finished he had a two-foot strand of fishing line with loops tied in each end. With one end clenched in his teeth and the other over his feet, he started rocking back and forth. The sawing motion started to cut through the nylon tie. Drops of blood dripped from his jaw as the abrasive line cut into his flesh, but he continued to saw back and forth. Finally, the tie popped, releasing his hands. He looked around for an easier method to cut the tie on his feet, and found a knife lying nearby. Free, Pagliano rubbed his hands, trying to get some circulation back as he peered over the gunwale and smiled.

He rolled over the side, knife in hand, and waded through the calf-deep water to the shore. It didn't take any tracking skills to follow the footprints in the sand. His scar throbbed as his anger built. No one, especially not a punk like Cody Braken was going to treat Joey Pagliano like that. And the way the girl had sneered at him. They were all going in the tank — the whole damned family. Carefully, he moved the mangrove branches out of his way, staying low and moving slowly — stalking them. The clearing came into view and he squatted behind a dense clump of mangroves. The tangled web of branches made an excellent screen as he watched, though the mosquitos found him quickly. Within seconds there was a swarm around him. It took every ounce of patience not to swat at them. He listened to the conversation of the four Brakens surrounding the tank.

"Do you even know what's in those buckets?" Nicole confronted Cody.

"I'm gonna trust that our friend Joey knows how to get rid of evidence." He opened a lid. "Smells like fertilizer. I bet he's got a bomb brewing in here."

"Great, Cody. Now that we got away from him, you're going to blow us all up," she said. Thunder boomed in the background causing her to look at the darkening sky.

"Shut up, Nicole. Dad, Matt help me dump these in the hole." The only way to clear his family was to destroy the tank with Joey Pagliano in it. He went toward the lid. "Used to be a crowbar around here somewhere." He started searching around the tanks, kicking at fallen brush.

Pagliano sat and watched as Cody found the crowbar and, with the help of Braken and Matt, pried the lid off the tank. He almost laughed out loud as Braken and Matt gagged from the smell. Nicole was spared, as she stood off to the side, upwind of the tank. *Might as well let them do all my work for me,* he thought, as they emptied the buckets into the hole. Cody picked up a tiki torch and dug in his pocket for something to light the fuse with. He came up empty and looked at Braken, who handed him an old zippo. The fuse ignited and Cody tossed the entire lamp in the tank. Nothing happened. Pagliano watched as he picked up a container of acetone and held it up as if to read the label.

"Come on now. Just dump it in and finish the job*," Pagliano said under his breath.*

As if on cue, Cody opened the jug and started pouring the contents into the pit. He jumped back as smoke started to stream from the opening, the wind blowing it towards the group. They covered their heads as another thunderclap let loose, closer this time.

"What the hell, Cody?" Nicole gagged and went for the other jugs. "You have any idea what you're doing?" She had to scream over the building wind, "Your son is here. Are you going to blow him up too?" She grabbed for Matt and moved away from the smoke, "Idiot," she muttered.

"She's right," Braken intervened. "We need to deal with Pagliano before we dump the rest in. Let's go get him and end this."

"Grandpa! Dad! You can't kill the man. That's what the police are for."

Braken turned to Nicole. "Take him away from here. He doesn't need to see this."

Pagliano ducked low as Braken and Cody went past him following the path to the boat. He only had a few minutes before they would find that he had escaped. Once they were out of sight, he started to move through the mangroves. The mosquitos were suspiciously absent now, like they could sense what was about to happen, as the storm closed in.

He saw Nicole and Matt ahead. Crouching, he moved closer, as they stood there in each other's arms, Matt trying to comfort her. The boy was the key. He doubted Nicole had much fight left in her after the abuse she'd already taken. She'd fold as soon as the boy was gone.

He went into a sprinter's stance and sprang from the bushes. Matt was in his arms, knife at his neck, before either one knew what had happened. He pursed his lips as if to whisper, letting Nicole know not to scream, or the boy would die. The knife was close to drawing blood as he applied more pressure, and he started to move it back and forth when the bushes stirred. Braken and Cody emerged empty handed and out of breath. A quick step back and he had Matt out of sight

"Pagliano's gone! Where's Matt?" Braken frantically checked the clearing.

"Pagliano's got him," she yelled.

* * *

"Look, it's Scarface," Sheryl yelled.

Will turned from his focus on the boat ahead and followed her gaze, watching a lone figure enter the mangroves. "You sure? I saw a man, but couldn't tell who it was."

"I'm sure. They're all gone."

Will idled alongside Cody's boat. It was empty. "Keep an eye on the island, I'm going to hop on and see if I can figure out what they're up to." He put the boat in neutral, went forward, and opened a hatch. A coiled dock line in hand, he went to the center of the boat, and tied the boats together. Thunder boomed again bringing a cool gust with it, indicating the storm was about to hit. He climbed from boat to boat and once aboard the Grady-White, he quickly searched the cabin and came back onto the deck. Two metal containers, about a gallon each, caught his attention.

"Acetone!" she saw the labels first.

"We've got to do something. They're going to blow the whole tank. Those buckets they were carrying - it's starting to make sense."

"Where's the sheriff? I called and told them Braken was headed here," she said, checking the horizon.

"I don't see them. We have to at least try and save Matt and stop them from blowing this up." Will said.

"But it's just the two of us and we're unarmed."

"We'll have to use the element of surprise," he said.

He sniffed the increasing wind like a dog. "Storm's getting close. If we go around to the other side of the island, we can beach the boat and see what they're up to. From that direction the wind will cover any sound we make. Why don't you try the sheriff again and see where they are. Tell them we're just going to take a look."

She picked up the phone to call as thunder boomed again.

"Storms done something to the signal. It's dead."

He shook his head as he untied the boats and tossed the dock line on the deck, then went to the wheel, pushed forward on the throttle and steered back toward the point. Once around the bend, he turned the wheel toward a clear section of beach. Another loud boom from the thunderhead, now almost directly above them let loose and he used the cover to gun the motor, disguising its noise. The first raindrops met them as they hopped out of the beached boat and onto the sand.

"This is only going to help us," she said, looking up at the sky.

His eyes followed her eyes, and he nodded in agreement. The sound of the rain and wind would disguise them, as well as making their prey less wary. They crossed the short beach and entered the mangroves, staying just clear of the trail that led toward the tanks.

Unarmed and unsure of what lay ahead, he moved inland. The storm increased in intensity disguising their awkward movements. It was raining so hard he could barely see. Branches slapped their faces and they stumbled over roots as they plowed forward through the brush. A flash of lightning and gust of wind took him by surprise and he went down. He assumed it was another root, but lightning flashed again and he saw the scar-faced man hovering above him, knife extended overhead ready to strike. The next thing he knew, he was face down in the muddy sand.

* * *

Will rolled over, his face covered with mud. He wiped his eyes off and looked to his side. Scarface was prone on the ground, Sheryl standing over both of them with a piece of driftwood. The last thing he remembered was falling, thinking he had landed on Sheryl, but he had run into Scarface. She must have hit him in the head. As the pieces came together Matt ran past him into Nicole's arms. Cody started towards them, anger in his eyes.

"Will, Look out!" Sheryl screamed, moving ahead of him brandishing the driftwood.

Cody ignored them and went for Pagliano.

"Freeze!" Braken walked up to the group pointing a small gun. "Everybody is going to calm down." He looked at Cody, "Drag him over there and toss him in," he pointed the gun at Pagliano. "And finish the tank off. Then we'll get out of here."

Cody didn't hesitate. He grabbed Pagliano's feet and started to drag him through the mud toward the tank. Just as he reached the edge of the tank, a knife flashed out and slashed him behind the heel. The blade tore through his Achilles tendon, causing him to fall. His momentum took him toward the open tank lid. He caught himself on the lip, but Pagliano hovered over him, knife in hand, rain water dripping from him. Cody grabbed his ankle, trying to stem the pain and blood flow, when the knife came down again, this time taking him deep in the shoulder.

Will and Sheryl stood side by side knowing as long as Braken had the gun there was nothing they could do. He still had the barrel pointed at them while he watched the action unfold. Seeing Cody go down, Braken swung the gun and fired a shot that buried itself in the sand by Pagliano's head. Matt ran towards his grandfather causing another bullet to miss its mark and ricochet off the concrete tank.

"Stop shooting. You're going to hit Dad!"

Will saw the opportunity as soon as the barrel swung away. He reached down for the piece of wood Sheryl had dropped and went towards Braken striking a hard blow to his head. The older man went down, dropping the gun in the sand. Will grabbed the gun and went for the tank but was too late. As he approached, Pagliano kicked Cody in the stomach, causing him to fold over and drop into the tank.

* * *

Matt screamed when Cody disappeared. Without thinking, he rushed toward Pagliano, taking him by surprise and knocking him off balance. They fell together and in a rage, Matt grabbed Pagliano's head and slammed it into the concrete. The body went limp, but he continued to slam the head until a hand grasped his shoulder.

He looked up and saw Will standing over him trying to control him, but fueled by adrenaline and anger, he resisted. The rest of the group was closing in on him. Before they could get to him, he let out a primal scream and shoved Pagliano into the tank.

Then, he felt hands dragging him away from the opening.

The next few minutes were a blur, as the clearing filled with people. Flashlight beams were moving everywhere. Finally he felt like he reentered his body, and took in the scene. Police were everywhere, and his grandfather was talking to a woman who appeared to be the sheriff. Will and Sheryl stood off to the side, watching. He panicked, not seeing his mother, but then felt a reassuring squeeze on his shoulder, and turned to find her behind him.

They stood there holding each other, watching the scene unfold. Braken was off to the side being tended to by a medic while the sheriff talked to Will and Sheryl. He caught a smile from Will and returned it. The rain continued, but with less intensity. Two deputies were working to get Pagliano out of the tank. They had a life ring from their boat lowered and were encouraging the semi-conscious man to climb into it. They finally had him on the ground where a medic went to him while the other deputies started to probe the tank for Cody.

When she was done interviewing Will and Sheryl the sheriff guided the three Brakens out of the clearing and down the path toward her boat.

"I'll take you back in and make sure you get checked out," she said to Nicole. "Then I'm going to need your statement. The boat you came here on is part of the crime scene."

"What about Matt? Is he in trouble? That was an evil man," Nicole asked.

"There's no reason that good people need to get dragged down by this," she reassured them. She pointed at Will and Sheryl who were climbing onto the flats boat, "They told me what happened."

Pagliano was propped between the two deputies as they escorted him to one of the sheriff's boats. Matt shivered as he glared at them.

"What about him?" Matt asked.

"He's going to be locked away for a long time," Jules said, "You don't need to worry about him."

But Matt was not reassured.

Before he could speak Nicole cut him off, "Cody?"

"They're pulling his body out now. He's alive but needs attention. I called in for a helicopter to evacuate him. We'll just have to wait and see."

Matt breathed a long sigh, shivering, and letting the tension go.

"Thank you," Nicole said as they reached the edge of the clearing. Two sheriff's boats bobbed at anchor in the chop, one pulled anchor and headed in as they boarded the inflatable beached in front of them.

Once on the larger boat, Matt didn't look back as they shot over the waves toward shore. He focused on the boat in front with Pagliano.

* * *

The wind had died by half just after the line of storms blew through, scrubbing the air and leaving clear skies. The first cold front of the season was upon them, the stripe of clouds visible in the moonlight marking its edge to the west. Two-foot seas, driven by the North wind were coming from behind them making the ride more comfortable than the wet bashing they had taken on the way out here.

They sat next to each other holding hands, lost in their own thoughts until Will rounded the point and entered the canal leading to the marina. The adrenaline was fading and he yawned.

"Not exciting enough for you?" she broke the silence.

"Just wondering what to do for a second date," he said.

Epilogue

The setting sun reflected off their glasses as Will and Sheryl toasted. They sat on his deck, looking out over the pristine waters. Far to the north was Flamingo Key, a thin line, barely visible above the water.

"Congratulation," Sheryl said, sipping her champagne.

"Thanks, but I couldn't have done it without you," Will said. He had gotten the final on the house today, mainly through her encouragement and connections with the building department. It had been a hard-fought few months, and he was exhausted from running charters during the day and working on the house at night. It was done enough for now.

They sat in silence for a few minutes, before she spoke. "Did you see the paper today?"

He shook his head.

"Braken was indicted. They pulled his Real Estate license too."

"I'll drink to that," Will said, raising his glass. "Cody's supposed to be down in Key West, working as a mate for one of the charter captains. It's nice at the marina without him around. I kind of miss Matt, though."

Cody had tried to make a go of it after the incident and had even been better with Matt and Nicole. Only the senior Broken and Pagliano had faced charges. Cody had walked away relatively unscathed, but his rehabilitation had exposed him to painkillers, which he gulped regularly.

Will's recent success running snapper and grouper trips had

irked him too. His once lucrative charter business with his father bringing him customers and the pipe providing limits of fish was gone. He had lost his secret hole when the County filled the old septic tanks and removed the drainage line.

"That mobster guy still worries me," Sheryl said.

"I think that guy's long gone. Besides the warrants out for his arrest, he sticks out here. If he's still in the country, I bet it's Jersey or Miami." Will too, had looked over his shoulder for weeks after Pagliano disappeared.

The wounds had healed, and with the final inspection approved, he could relax and go back to catch and release charters.

He looked over at the one thing that had gone right for him, but she was no longer smiling. The talk had put a frown on Sheryl's face. "I'll be right back," he said, rising from the chair.

It was dark now, and he stood beside the switch. "Ready?"

"Ready for what?" she asked, turning toward him.

Holding his breath, he flicked the switch on and the house lit up.

"Oh, my god. You got power!" Sheryl jumped up.

Will smiled. "Turned on today, after the paperwork went through.

"That's awesome."

He hesitated. A lot of thought had gone into his next question. "So, now that the place is livable and legal how about we share it?"

She jumped up and went for him. "I would have without all this."

"I know, but I had to prove some stuff to myself first."

"You did that a long time ago for me. Of course, I will," she said and embraced him

Thanks For Reading

If you liked the book please leave a review:
Leave a Review Here

For more information please check out my web page:
https://stevenbeckerauthor.com/

Or follow me on Facebook:
https://www.facebook.com/stevenbecker.books/

Sign up for my newsletter
Click or enter the address below
Get Wood's Ledge for FREE!
mactravisbooks.com

[Image: view.jpg]

While tarpon fishing in the backcountry of the Florida Keys, Mac Travis discovers a plot to drill for oil in the pristine waters.

Also by Steven Becker

Mac Travis Adventures
Wood's Relic
Wood's Reef
Wood's Wall
Wood's Wreck
Wood's Harbor
Wood's Reach
Wood's Revenge (February 2017)
Tides of Fortune
Pirate
The Wreck of the Ten Sail
Haitian Gold
Will Service Thrillers
Bonefish Blues
Tuna Tango
Dorado Duet (December 2016)
Storm Series
Storm Rising

Made in the USA
San Bernardino, CA
03 December 2018